LEGENDS OF THE PHOENIX

WRITTEN BY C S NOCTON

Order this book online at www.trafford.com/07-2612
or email orders@trafford.com

Most Trafford titles are also available at major online book retailers.

Note for Librarians: A cataloguing record for this book is available from Library and Archives Canada at www.collectionscanada.ca/amicus/index-e.html

This book is printed on recycled paper.
ISBN: 978-1-4251-5799-9

We at Trafford believe that it is the responsibility of us all, as both individuals and corporations, to make choices that are environmentally and socially sound. You, in turn, are supporting this responsible conduct each time you purchase a Trafford book, or make use of our publishing services. To find out how you are helping, please visit www.trafford.com/responsiblepublishing.html

Our mission is to efficiently provide the world's finest, most comprehensive book publishing service, enabling every author to experience success. To find out how to publish your book, your way, and have it available worldwide, visit us online at www.trafford.com/10510

www.trafford.com

North America & international
toll-free: 1 888 232 4444 (USA & Canada)
phone: 250 383 6864 ♦ fax: 250 383 6804 ♦ email: info@trafford.com

The United Kingdom & Europe
phone: +44 (0)1865 722 113 ♦ local rate: 0845 230 9601
facsimile: +44 (0)1865 722 868 ♦ email: info.uk@trafford.com

10 9 8 7 6 5 4 3 2

Preface

Hello reader, my name is Christopher Stephen Nocton and this is my first ever book. I come from Huddersfield in West Yorkshire, England and am a graduate of the University of Huddersfield. Since leaving university I was unsure of where I wanted to go with my career but for a long time I had a storyline running through my head. One day I decided it would be a good idea to write it down and from then on the writing snowballed into a potential series of books entitled 'Legends Of The Phoenix' the first of which you are reading now. This book introduces the principle character of Dan Wild who the books are based on. This book and future series are a culmination of three years work and I am proud to say I have finally got the first book into print. Hopefully you will find it as interesting to read as I have in creating it. Maybe in a few years you could be reading some more of my work; I hope so. Thank you for reading this book and enjoy!

Dedications

This is the hard part for me remembering to thank all the people who have made this possible for me and the positive and sometimes negative influences that have help shape Legends Of The Phoenix (LOTP). First and foremost I would like to thank God for giving me this wonderful gift to pour out my heart in this medium which excites me so much having created my own little world.

Secondly I want to thank Sophia for all her beautiful designs. When I asked Sophia to paint me a picture of a Phoenix for my 21st birthday I was overwhelmed by the gift that arrived at my house. This picture has now become the centre piece for the LOTP book providing an eye catching front cover and has given me much motivation when looking at it for story writing. I would also like to give a huge thank you out to Graham for his mentoring with this project and my life in general. I have gained some positive experiences from our time together and want to give him and his wife Julie a heart felt thank you for all the times they have opened up their door to me in order to give me the opportunity to get LOTP to this stage.

I would like to thank all my friends especially those who have given me advice and constructive criticism and thank you all for telling me what you really think rather than telling me what I think I need to hear. It makes me cringe sometimes when I say 'please be honest with me' but people have said things in a helpful way that has facilitated my redevelopment of the work I had done to the point where I can now say I have written my own book! That's quite a scary thought actually.

And finally I would like to thank my family because lets

face it where would I be without them. To Mum, Dad, Angie, Uncle Stephen and Grandma I hope this is something that you can be proud of and that there are many more to come. Thank you all, Chris.

Table of Contents

SECTION 02

SECTION 03

LEGENDS OF THE PHOENIX

SECTION 01
Timing

The story begins with a group of seven sat around a table having a discussion. The language they are speaking is not one of Earth. Cloaks hide their faces and bodies. It is a heated discussion lead by the group member sitting in the middle.

Member 1: "It is time we sent for the boy."

Member 2: "No, he must not come until we are sure it is him and the signs tell us when to burn the sacrifice."

Member 1: "Our operatives on Earth tell us this is the boy. They are positive. The proper tests have been carried out and he shall be the one if we send for him now."

Member 3: "But what about the signs?"

Member 4: "We have had enough signs to know that it is the right time. There is only one that has not revealed itself to us."

Member 5: "Then we should wait until it does."

Member 6: "You know how some are hard to decipher. We could be missing our opportunity waiting for a sign to appear when it is already happening."

Leader: "Silence. We shall not waste time any longer. We will put it to the vote. Who believes we should go ahead with the plan now?" They are interrupted as a door opens and a silhouette is shone through the room.

Leader: "Yes? What is it?"

Silhouette: "The last sign sires, it has come to pass." The leader leans forward.

Leader: "Are you sure? Has it been checked?"

Silhouette: "Yes my Lord it is what we have been waiting for." The silhouette leaves the room and the leader finishes the meeting.

Leader: "It is settled then. Do what must be done." They nod their heads and all but one leaves him. "Our fates are sealed. It will be interesting to see how this turns out. Send the eyes."

England, Earth

A young boy, about seven years old is chasing his dog out of the house one night. He is not far from his home when his parents call him back. As he is returning to the house he notices a light in the sky. He calls his parents over to where he is to have a look.

Boy: "Mum, Dad, come and look at this."

Mother: "What is it Dan?" she asks and then looks to where he is pointing in the sky. "George, what is that?"

George: "It's… well I'm not sure but it looks to be coming this way." The light is actually a fireball hurtling towards them from space. The two of them look at each other. They notice it is heading right for them and start running towards the house. "I think it could be a meteor, quick Patricia get back inside."

Patricia: "Lets get into the basement; hopefully we'll be safe down there."

Dan's parents make it to the front porch but he goes back for his dog, which is in the road barking at the oncoming light. The fireball hits the two of them dead on. It then bounces back up into space leaving the charred bones and burning flesh of the dog but no other sign it was there. Dan's parents, filled with emotion, run to the road to find only the remains of the dog.

The Cave

The flame enters the atmosphere of a planet. As it moves, it plunges downwards, passing over a forest of very dense woodland, which shows no signs of civilisation. Lights can be seen in the dark from a clearing and from a cave in a mountain where a figure sees the flame and rushes back inside.

Sacrificial Area

At the foot of the Snowy Mountains on the far outskirts of the City of Shonrar, there is a large bonfire in front of a rocky slope with lots of villagers dancing around chanting. The chief of the village sits on a wooden throne in view of a platform where a young boy is tied to a post, waiting to be sacrificed. The blonde haired boy looks down in front of him where there is a burning casket. He is gagged, but starts to squirm and scream under it as he looks up and sees a flame in the sky, approaching them. The rest of the villagers stop chanting and watch as the flame heads towards them. The chief, a young boy himself, looks away from the casket he has been staring at with a tear in his eye, puts on a brave face and stands up amidst a troop of guards to say something to those around him, who all begin to cheer. A woman with dark black hair appears behind him on his platform. She looks up the rock face to some villagers who are diverting the flow of water coming from a cliff ledge away from the altar situated below them.

The flame hits the sacrificial altar where the boy is tied up and burns it to the ground as the group surrounding it watch on. After a nod from the chief, the villagers on the cliff face let some of the water flow to douse the flames. The villagers below wait till the smoke has died down then go towards the rubble.

They start to dig with their hands and in the middle of the rubble they find the blonde boy's burnt fleshy skeleton. They continue to dig, even though the ashes are still hot. Then they find Dan's body amongst the remnants. The villagers begin cheering again as the dark haired woman goes with the chief over to the boy. She immediately checks him out to find he is not breathing. He has drowned under the water from above, but she manages to revive him. Dan stares up at the commotion as the two of them stand above him. He then passes out but sees an upset soldier standing by some trees with some of his colleagues, looking bruised and battered, before his head hits the ground. He is moved away from the altar as the rest of the fire is put out. The casket has burnt away. The only remaining lights are those of torches erected around the site. As the fire is extinguished the torches flare up and the villagers turn to face the woods with their backs towards the rocks. Noises start coming from the woods and the villagers begin running around in a mad panic. At the command of the chief, they then head for some caves in the mountainside. Some go past the outskirts of the sacrificial area where the torches have been laid and are pulled kicking and screaming through the foliage. The chief points at a stretcher and two of his guards place Dan onto it and carry him to the caves. All the villagers that have not been taken follow them into the cave. A few torches are left at the entrance and the villagers start moving more slowly through the course of manmade tunnels. As they progress through the cave they can hear the sounds of the beasts gathering outside the tunnel. The beasts do not come too close because they are afraid of the light. For this reason none of the villagers have a good description of them because the only ones to have seen them fully are their victims, just before they are killed.

Mountain Cave

From his vantage point in a cave up in the mountains, the lonely figure watches as the lights in the sacrificial area are knocked out.

"He's dead. We will bring you his bones when we have finished with the torches." The man doesn't move as the voice of a shadow being creeps up behind him. He is saddened, but unafraid as it emerges beside him. "Milo, are you listening? The deal you made with my master still stands. You have immunity from us and we will help you avenge his death."

Milo: "The other? Is it alive?"

Shadow: "From what we could see, but barely. If you could do something before the new healer, Alemap, gets her hands on it then…"

Milo: "No", he shouts. He turns to the shadow being who bows his head as Milo passes to return into the cave. The shadow then scowls when he isn't looking. "I cannot enter that village any more, you know that. I am too well known and the villagers must know I am up to something if I go in. I would probably be killed on sight."

Shadow: "What would you have us do?"

Milo: "Nothing right now, it's too close to morning. Go back to your kind. I will think of some way to get my revenge." The shadow turns to leave. "Make sure you get all the body though and try to bring it back in as few a pieces as possible."

Shadow: "Very well." He leaves.

Milo: "I need it." He says to himself.

The Village

The Laboratory

Dan begins to come around and finds himself in what looks like a laboratory. He is lying on the stretcher that the guards brought him in on. He sits up and looks around. He has fear in his eyes as he wonders what they are going to do with him. No one is in the room, but he can see two guards with their backs turned to him outside the door. Dan slowly walks round the room, trying to be quiet. He has no escape from the room he is in, so he proceeds into the corridor leading to the next room. It is not fully lit but Dan can see some surgical equipment on a trolley near the door. He slowly heads towards it, passing lots of curtains and looking for something sharp he can use to defend himself. He finds a few objects and places them in his pocket. As he is picking up a scalpel he accidentally knocks some of the equipment on the floor.

"Who is making all that noise?" A grumpy voice says. A light comes on and one of the curtains next to him is pulled back as something not human sits up in bed and stares towards Dan. In a panic, Dan throws the scalpel towards the being but misses. The being shouts for help as the scalpel hits the wall behind him and then falls next to him on his bed. The guards come rushing in. Dan turns to see them running towards him. He turns back and runs past the bed of the being, knocking over the trolley. He stops suddenly in his tracks, falling backwards to the ground as other lights come on and he sees more of what appear to be monsters popping their heads out from behind curtains.

A human looking lady enters the room. "What's going on here?" she demands. Dan turns to look at her but he can't see her because she is standing in the doorway where the guards were posted and the light from behind her just casts a shadow.

Being 1: "This thing just tried to kill me Matron. I just woke up and it's standing there with a knife, look." He agitatedly cries and points to the scalpel in the bed. The woman walks into the room and the doors close behind her. "He's the human, he doesn't understand yet." Dan looks at her face. He feels a twinge in his arm and then his eyes open wide and he feels scarred as he is shown images and sounds of when he first got out of the rubble. He recognises the woman as the lady who was standing there when he was resuscitated, although her attire is completely different, more professional and less threatening. The images end and Dan returns to the room. The woman looks over at him. "What happened to you?" Her tone had softened as she talked to him. Dan looked down at his arm and lifted up his sleeve to find something like a weird looking watch attached to him. He tried to take it off but the woman stopped him.

Woman: "You saw something, didn't you? Good, I'm glad it's working."

Dan: "What is it? Get it off me."

Woman: "We need you to leave it on for now…" he pulls it off and she begins speaking in another language. She puts it back on him. "Can you understand me now?"

Dan: "Yes."

Woman: "You need to leave it on so you can understand what I'm saying. Come. We will go somewhere a bit quieter." She turns towards the guards.

"Clean that up and put them back to bed." She held out her hand to help Dan off the floor; he reluctantly accepted. She escorted him out of the room, leading with her hand on his shoulder.

Alemap's Office

Dan: "Where are my Mum and Dad?"

Woman: "They're not here. I need you to be brave now because you may not see them again." Dan begins to sob quietly as she sits him on a couch.

Dan: "What? Why? Where are they? Where am I?"

Woman: "Don't worry, we're going to do the best we can to make sure that doesn't happen. We want to send you home, but in order for that to happen you have to do a few things for us."

Dan: "We? Who are you?"

Woman: "I'm sorry, where are my manners? My name is Alemap. I am the new head healer here in Shonrar, in Jenon. I don't know what they are called on your world."

Dan: "My world? Well, where are we now, Mars?" Alemap begins to laugh. She reaches over to her desk and hands him a tissue.

Alemap: "No, Mars is a long way from Phosia where we are right now. You took the long way to get here because you didn't have one of those devices on your arm." She sits on the couch next to him.

Dan: "What is it?"

Alemap: "It's what we call a Hader. It has many uses." She leans in closer "one of them is to help get you home, but it won't work just yet."

Dan: "When will it work then? I want to go home now..." he demanded as his sadness began to turn to anger.

Alemap: "I'd love to send you but I can't, so how about we get you something to eat? You must be hungry by now. You can have whatever you want and later we shall have another little chat, but right now we must join the others in a celebratory feast." She stands up and heads towards the door. "Come on then."

Dan: "What are we celebrating?" He asked, feeling hungry.

Alemap: "You!" They leave the room together. As they proceed down the corridor, Dan enquires, "You're not going to eat me are you?" Alemap laughs, "No of course not silly, you're the guest of honour."

The Lookout

Dan waits in the corridor behind the door, where the guards are watching over as Alemap changes into a celebration outfit she has in her office. As he waits, he looks out of what appears to be a window in the wall. It is all black so he goes to investigate. As he goes to touch it, Alemap emerges through the door and pulls him back. "You don't want to do that at this time of night or we could all be in danger."

Dan: "Why?"

Alemap: "Because if there are spies outside looking for us, you could give our location away. Hold on." She goes and turns out the light and then touches the glass on the stone wall. As she touches it, the glass disappears. Dan feels the fresh air on his face, but he can't see anything much. As Dan glances out of the window, Alemap pulls back some leaves and branches to reveal a great forest down below them. Dan gasps at the sheer beauty of the moon-drenched forest. "You see that waterfall down there?" She points to their left, where a small waterfall leads into a stream. "That's where I live."

Dan: "Where, I don't see any houses?"

Alemap: "I'll show you later, as for now we must go." They head off to the feast. When they get outside Dan can't see very much because clouds are covering the moon. They walk to a carriage outside and get in. Dan looks to the front as he steps up into the carriage and sees that there isn't a horse, but the head of a creature he's never seen before. It looks like a bird in the face, but has a large cat like body. It blows cold air out of its nostrils. As they sit in silence, Dan watches the trees passing by and then looks over to Alemap. She is quite a slender lady, with long dark hair which she wears tied up for the event.

Dan: "That's a nice outfit. Am I a little underdressed?"

Alemap: "No, trust me, you'll be fine wearing that for now."

Dan: "Can I ask? How old are you?"

Alemap: "I'm seventeen. Why?"

Dan: "And your job is what?"

Alemap: "The village healer. I've just finished my training, well, most of it. We were kind of in a desperate situation for another healer after the last one ran off. It's all new having the responsibility, but I'm loving it and I have plenty of sources if I need help, plus a great medical staff."

The Feast

In what looks to be a cave with multiple tunnels, a grand spread of food and drink are laid out for the returning tribe, who have all changed into their celebratory clothes. It is a solemn occasion and even those who were weeping over the losses of their loved ones attend. A head table sits with its back to the cave wall, from which all the tunnels can be seen. The head table seats nine of the Shonrar leaders and looks out at the several tables spread before them, each seating about twenty. There are two empty seats in the middle of the head table. Guards are posted around the room at all the tunnel entrances.

The Speech

A guard whispers into the ear of the man sitting next to the empty chair, directly in the centre of the table. He stands up and takes a jug in his hand. The man sitting next to him rolls his eyes. He begins to speak "Don't worry Christian, this will be my best speech yet."

Christian mutters, "That's what I'm afraid of."

The speaker addresses the hungry looking mass before him, "Jenoans of Phosia. I, Maddox, proud to be a Jenoan this day…" He starts waving around his jug and Christian begins to cringe, "…am deeply saddened by the loss of our loved ones. Tomorrow we will go and retrieve the bodies of those loved ones who didn't make it back." He pauses for a moment, "Tonight, however, we shall celebrate their lives and the contributions they have made to this so noble a cause." His actions begin to get more forceful and the drink from the jug starts wetting Christian. The rest of those at the table begin to giggle but try to hide the fact. A guard standing next to one of the tunnels nods to Maddox. He continues, "And now would you please all stand for the arrival of Lord Stephen." Lord Stephen, the young ruler of Jenon, walks from the tunnel entrance with an escort of guards to take his place at the empty centre seat.

After applause, he gestures to the crowd to sit down. A waiter comes and refills Maddox's jug and provides Christian with a couple of napkins to wipe himself. Lord Stephen begins to speak, "My friends, it has been a hard time for us lately with the death of my father and now the slaughter of more of his subjects. Those of us who are left can now do what he could not; drive these evil forces from our land and reclaim Jenon as our own. I have what my father only dreamed of; the weapon we can use against the enemy." They begin to cheer.

The guard nods to Maddox again whom immediately stands up. He whispers into the Lord's ear "He's here now. I'll take over." Lord Stephen sits down and the Jenoans clap again.

Maddox: "And now here he is the guest of honour… what's he called?" Those around him shrug and shake their heads. So Maddox just puts his arm out towards Dan and smiles. Dan is led thought the tunnel entrance to the table by guards. Alemap enters the room and Lord Stephen sits up in his seat. Dan approaches the table and Maddox asks him his name. "It's Dan, Dan Wild, sir."

Maddox: "Dan, Dan Wild ladies and gentlemen!" A little over excited he spills the rest of his drink down Christian. A waiter comes over with a towel for him.

Lord Stephen: "Bring him a chair" he demands. "Come sit here with me, you must be hungry." Dan sits next to him on the chair provided on Lord Stephen's right, with Alemap taking the last available chair on the opposite side of him. Lord Stephen continues, "The food you requested is here now."

A waiter put his request on the table in front of him. "What is it?" Lord Stephen asks.

Dan: "Where I come from, it's what we call tomato soup and bread."

Lord Stephen: "I know what bread is," he laughs. "So you pour this tomato soup into your bread to make a sandwich?"

Dan: "No, you dip the bread in the soup like this." He shows them. Lord Stephen clicks his fingers and a waiter comes over to him.

Lord Stephen: "I'll try some of this tomato soup." The waiter brings him some and some bread.

Dan: "Careful it's hot."

Lord Stephen: "Yes, it's nice…" he says to his friends sitting beside him. "…You should try some. In fact everyone should try some! Bring out tomato soup and bread for everyone."

Dan: "You can also break up the bread into pieces and put it in the bowl and then eat it with a spoon." They all watch avidly at the spectacle the young boy is providing.

Falcons & Leaders

After the meal, Lord Stephen, who is only a few years older than Dan, turns to him and says, "I think we shall have that soup at the beginning of every feast. Now you have a few things you must attend to." Looking more official, he says, "Go stand at the front of the table there. Christian?"

Christian: "Yes my Lord."

Lord Stephen: "Send for the boys." Nine boys enter the room led by Christian who then goes back to his seat. They stand in a line in front of the table, facing the men and Alemap before them. They too are Dan's age and are behind him. Dan doesn't know whether to look round or not, so looks to Lord Stephen and Alemap for instructions. Lord Stephen continues "Dan who would you like to be your council?" he asks, gesturing to those at the table. Dan looks confused.

Dan: "What do you mean?"

Lord Stephen: "Who do you want to look after you while you are here? You can pick anyone."

Dan: "How about you?"

Lord Stephen: "I'm sorry, but I'll be too busy taking care of official matters, I won't have time. Choose someone else."

Dan: "Alemap?" She rushes over to Lord Stephen to state her dislike about the situation but he soon puts her straight. "You know as well as I, that whoever he chooses must be his council throughout his stay here. Anyone, that is, who isn't my family or me. It is what the prophecy says."

Alemap: "But I've just started as a carer at the hospital, you know it's what I've been wanting to do for ages."

Lord Stephen: "You can still do it part time but your main concern should be the caring of him." She takes in a deep breath and agrees. She sits next to Lord Stephen in Dan's chair. Lord Stephen turns to Dan. "Now you have chosen your council you will need to choose a partner with which to train."

Dan: "Train for what?"

Lord Stephen: "That will be revealed to you later. Right now, choose one of these whom you wish to be your partner. Choose wisely, because the only way to change him is if he dies." Dan looks worried. He walks up and down the line. "Each of the boys has different skills and you shall all work as a team." Lord Stephen continues. Dan notices a boy with his head down, muttering "Please don't be me, please don't be me…" while the others stand proudly.

Lord Stephen: "The two of you shall …"

Dan: "I choose him", he interrupts pointing to the shy boy.

Maddox: "Well done Mal, I'm so proud of you!"

Mal: "Thanks Dad", he says looking quite worried.

Dan: "Dad?"

Mal: "Yes, we are all the sons of the men you see before you, apart from Chris…I mean Lord Stephen, obviously."

Dan: "Where's his father?"

Mal: "He died just recently", he said with a solemn face. "Anyway, we are their sons, given the best training in…"

Christian: "Well my lad, I think it's time to go to bed. Off you go with Alemap. Mal and the others will see you tomorrow bright and early."

Dan: "Why what's happening tomorrow?"

Christian: "You find out."

Alemap: "Come on, let's go."

Dan follows Alemap and hears how disappointed the other boys are until Maddox starts shouting how happy he is.

Alemap's Home

The next morning Dan awakes to find himself in a brightly lit room accompanied by the faint sound of running water.

Alemap: "Good morning. Did you sleep well?"

Dan: "Yes, I slept fine, where are we? How did I get here?"

Alemap: "You're in a place called Phosia, my name is Alemap…"

Dan: "Yes, I remember that bit but I don't remember how I got here. We were at the feast…" his wrist starts to twinge again and he is taken back into his memory, viewing the situations like they were happening to him right there, except he can't change anything and he knows it is a memory, rather than an experience. "…I had to choose two people, then we left and…"

Alemap: "OK, it's good that you're using your Hader, but we don't have time for this, you have to prepare for today." She gives him some breakfast. He looks around at Alemap's home. Christian arrives to take Dan, who is now dressed in Phosian clothing.

Dan: "Why? What's happening today?"

Alemap: "For a start you're going to train with the other boys until the scout comes back from checking the woods."

Dan: "Why?"

Alemap: "Because you have to go into the Shonrar woods with the others to retrieve the bodies of the 'people'…" she says, struggling with the word, "…who were killed last night." Don't worry, you will be safe; Christian and Maddox will be leading the soldiers, you boys just need to get the bodies onto the carts…"

The Courtyard

"…You will be helping us take the bodies to Lilechem where we will be…"

Dan, standing next to one of the other boys, whispers, "Where's Lilechem?" He gets a clout round the head.

Christian: "Listen up boys, your life could depend on it." He turns to face Dan "Lilechem is the capital of Jenon and is at the other side of the Shonrar woods." He begins to walk away then turns back and says "Oh, and if you have any more questions you ask me. Got it?"

Dan: "Yes, sir." Before Christian can open his mouth again, Dan has his hand in the air.

Christian: "Good! Now, where was I? Oh yes. You will not be fighting; you will not leave the side of the cart." He reaches the end of the line and turns back. "Yes Dan?"

Dan: "Why do we need to collect the dead bodies? It sounds a bit…" he doesn't know what the best word to describe the situation is, so he scrunches up his nose.

Christian: "Because if not the Boozemises may get you."

Dan: "What are Boozemises?" The other boys giggle.

Christian: "They are the bodies of the dead brought back to life. May I finish what I was saying now?" Dan nods. "If we are attacked, which is more than likely, then the cart shall stop and you must get under it. Remember to keep all body parts away from the wheels in case the griffins get spooked. What are you doing lad?" Dan holds his hand in the air. "I just want to know what a griffin is, sir?" He puts his hand down. The other boys begin to laugh.

Christian: "Now, now boys, Dan's not from around these parts."

Corey: "If they don't have griffins where you come from, how do you pull your carts?"

Dan: "With horses."

Corey: "Horses!" Christian slaps the boy round the head. "We don't have time for talking, the scout could be back at any time. Go put your uniforms on."

Dan: "I don't have a uniform."

Christian: "Don't worry, one has been provided for you in the barn over there. Now go, quick!"

After changing, the boys return to the courtyard. Christian and Maddox are discussing the trip.

Maddox: "Right then boys you will all have swords for fencing training." They all smile. Christian starts handing out the swords. "However, you will not be taking them with you." They all moan, "But, you will be issued with a dagger to use only in emergencies."

Christian: "And for cutting ropes, etc."

Maddox: "Yes, yes, quite right, but only to be used in emergencies when fighting. Otherwise you're likely to injure one another or have your weapon used against you."

Christian: "Now split up into pairs. Mal and Dan, you're together, everyone else choose your partners carefully, you will be working with each other from now on."

After half an hours training, the scout returns and informs them that enemy forces are still in the area and they should hold off a little longer. Christian and Maddox discuss the situation when Alemap arrives. She has come to see how Dan is progressing.

Maddox: "We don't know how many there are out there if we wait until tomorrow…"

Christian: "If we wait till tomorrow there maybe nothing left of our dead, they could be eaten or buried, or anything."

Maddox: "We don't want to endanger anymore of us."

Christian: "No, but if we don't go now, "You Know Who" could bring them back to life as Boozemises and the longer we leave it, the less time we have to get to Lilechem before dark."

Maddox: "Fine, but the scout leads the way, we take a different route and we take extra precautions."

Christian: "Such as what?"

Maddox: "We tell the boy…"

Alemap: "No, you will not tell him!"

Christian: "Alemap! Where did you come from?"

Alemap: "It's my responsibility to tell him. He needs to understand what's going to happen to him. If you tell him and he believes he is, you know, he might get himself hurt. The prophecy has begun but who knows how long it will be before we get him to full strength. It could be days, weeks, months or longer."

Maddox: "We won't say anything, we promise. Don't we?" They both turn to Christian. "Yes, yes, we won't say anything to… Dan!"

Dan: "Yes?" he asks, walking towards them.

Christian: "We were just going to look for you. Gather the boys, we're ready to go." Dan follows Christian's instructions immediately. He is a tall man of stocky build with a brown beard and speaks in a serious voice that commands respect, not only from Dan and the other boys, but from his peers also. Only a few don't seem in the slightest bit intimidated by him; Lord Stephen and the two standing with him are amongst those.

Maddox: "Say 'bye' to Alemap."

Alemap: "See you later. Be careful, do what the others tell you and don't listen to the stories the boys tell you. You'll have plenty of time to get used to this place."

Dan: "Why how long will I be here for?" She looked sympathetically towards him.

Alemap: "I don't know, but we'll have a chat when you return tomorrow afternoon. You won't be able to make it back before dark so you'll be staying overnight in Lilechem. Don't worry it's a very nice place and you can't find a better warrior in Jenon to protect you than Maddox here."

Dan: "OK, bye then."

The group sets off towards the woods. Maddox leads the patrol, with Christian bringing up the rear and twenty guards surrounding the cart either side. The boys sit in the cart admiring their new daggers, one apiece attached onto their belts. Maddox rides by the side of the cart for a moment. "Do you like your new daggers?" he asked the boys. They all were unanimous in saying yes. As Maddox was talking to them Dan noticed his shirt was undone part way and a silver necklace was hanging from his neck.

Mal: "That's a family heirloom. Supposedly, one of the wearers of the chain will unlock the answer to the problem they are seeking resolve for, when they are in their most needy hour. That's why we call it the key."

Shonrar Forest

As the patrol sets off towards the woods, Dan goes to sit by Mal in the back of the cart. He looks forward to see the same beasts that took him and Alemap to the feast, but this time the creatures were covered in armour on their heads and backs. There were two pulling the cart. Most of the guards were riding them and the rest walking alongside the cart. Dan looks to Mal. He is staring out at Christian. "What's wrong?" Dan asks.

Mal: "Why can't my Dad be like that?"

Dan: "What? Like Christian?"

Mal: "Yes, brave, a good swordsman, amongst other things. He's so courageous and confident." Maddox, who had ridden his griffin down to check everything was alright, hears the conversation the boys are having.

Dan: "Isn't your Dad good at all those things?"

Mal: "Yes, but he's also an embarrassment. You saw everyone laughing at him. I want a father who is respected like Christian; no one dares say anything bad about him." Maddox rides off back to the front line.

Dan: "You're so lucky."

Mal: "How's that?"

Dan: "You've got your Dad here with you now. My Dad's at home, probably thinking I'm dead. At least he's doing something to make you proud.

He's the top ranking warrior in Lord Stephen's army, from what Alemap has told me."

Mal: "I guess you're right."

Dan: "Don't be bothered about what they say they're only jealous."

Mal: "Thanks."

The Attack

The group have been travelling for twenty minutes. The kids are sitting on top of a pile of bodies they have collected along the way. There are only three more Jenoan's unaccounted for.

Suddenly one of the soldiers cries out. The group is under attack. "It's not Milo's men, it's Leychrians."

Dan: "What are Leychrians?"

Mal: "Enemies who live to the east of the Shonrar woods." The cart stops moving as Christian comes riding past on his griffin. "Boys, get under the cart NOW."

They all do as they are told and hide under the cart. The guards surround the cart and Christian rides up to Maddox to figure out their next move.

Maddox: "We've been followed for about three minutes. There was only one though so I didn't think much about it. I thought he was just checking we weren't heading into his territory, but it looks like he was at the back of the pack, not the front."

Christian: "How many are we looking at?"

Maddox: "I don't know but they definitely outnumber us."

Christian: "What do we do?"

Maddox: "There's only one thing we can do - fight. We're surrounded and we can't let them get their hands on the boy."

Christian: "Any of them."

Maddox: "Of course, but it's not just our futures he'll be sealing if he dies but the rest of Phosia and more. We must protect him with our lives. Once he gets to the right age he'll do the same for us. Protect the children, tell the guards to kill anything that attacks us. Don't attack unless they give you reason to."

Christian: "Where are you going?"

Maddox: "I'm going after the scout. Hopefully they won't have got their hands on him yet." Maddox rides off after the scout while Christian takes charge of the guards.

The group wait for their leaders return, keeping a close eye out for an attack. They cannot see their enemy but they can hear them and see movements in the foliage. The boys are underneath the cart facing in different directions in order to spot an enemy. Everyone is quiet apart from the racing of their heartbeats.

One of the guards notices something; rushes past a tree and points it out to Christian.

Christian: "So it ran past a tree, it's heading away from us over there."

Guard: "Yes sir, but it's left something on the tree, maybe a bit of clothing."

Christian: "Wait here." Christian goes to investigate; cautious it may be a trap. He looks at the item caught on a branch and his eyes grow larger when he realises what it is from. "Its troops from Leychr…run…" As he is shouting, he is pulled into a bush and sounds of a struggle ensue. No one dares move as they glance towards the bushes where their second in command was taken.

Dan: "I take it troops from Leychr are bad then?"

Mal: "Leychr, yes, they're cannibals."

Dan: "Cannibals!"

Mal: "Yes and the troops are worse than just regular Leychrians because they've been trained for battle."

Over in another part of the wood Maddox is still looking for the scout when he hears rustling in the trees and bushes. He looks up to find the scout hiding in a tree. "Maddox, its Leychrians" he says, "what are we going to do?" As he says this, three of them appear and drag him back into the bushes. Maddox knows he cannot do anything to save him as he hears the noises of his screams and mauling, so he sets about after the rest of the group. He is pushing aside some of the flaps on either side of his griffin's armour when he is surrounded by the beasts. They slowly start edging in towards him, when he rubs the bony looking areas on the griffin and wings begin to grow out of it.

Maddox flies back to group. He finds Christian hurt but alive. The rest of the guards are dead but the children have been taken alive to Rechly's castle. Maddox tells Christian they are ten minutes away from Lilechem, so they go there with the bodies and pick up the rest on the way.

Maddox: "At least we know we don't have to find the bodies of these guards, there won't be anything left but bones. We shall retrieve them on our return."

Christian: "First we need help from the Lilechem guards to get the children back."

Rechly's Castle

In Leychr, one Leychrian is pleased to take the spoils of the days hunt back to Rechly, the leader of the race in Jenon.

Teburnt: "Master, I have something for you."

Rechly: "What is it?"

Teburnt: "Jenoans."

Rechly: "Jenoans? Bring them to me" His eyes light up.

Teburnt: "They are here, Master."

Rechly: "Where are the adults, they are all children" he yells.

Teburnt: "They are in the woods, one of them is injured and the other…" he looks away.

Rechly: "The other?"

Teburnt: "He got away."

Rechly: "What?"

Teburnt: "It wasn't our fault, he…he flew away on a griffin."

Rechly: "You fool; those who ride griffins round these parts are well connected in the scheme of things."

Teburnt: "Sire, I don't think they were from the North but the South."

Rechly: "What were they doing?"

Teburnt: "They were collecting bodies."

Rechly: "Then it has begun. Stop the other two from reaching Lilechem; if they make it they will bring reinforcements."

Teburnt: "Can we have a snack now, Master? Just one?"

Dan, lined up with the others, involuntarily makes a noise in his throat.

Mal: "What is it?"

Dan: "Didn't you hear them; they said they are going to eat us?" He whispered.

Mal: "How can you understand what they are saying? Is Leychrian a language you speak where you come from?"

Dan: "No, it's this thing on my arm." He starts rolling up his sleeve.

Mal: "A Hader! Quick put it away. If they find out you have one of those, they might torture you for information if they know you speak the same language as them."

Dan: "But I don't speak their language."

Mal: "You do while you're wearing that. The thing with a Hader is that it translates any language in its database so you speak it or understand it. You don't even realise you are doing it. To you you're speaking your own language. Father and all the leaders at the table the other night have them. They have many uses, once you know how to activate them." Rechly notices the boys talking and creeps up beside them.

Dan: "It lets me access my memories and talk to you lot, what else can it do?"

Mal: "It can be used as a homing device so they can find us, presuming they know you have it. Also you can talk to anyone wearing one on Phosia, if you can get it to work."

Rechly: "Hello there, what would you two be talking about?" They boys look up a Rechly in fear.

Mal: "Don't say anything to them, if you do it'll translate it into their language."

Rechly: "Put them in the dungeon, but leave the noisy one. We're going to have something to eat boys."

Dan: "No, wait."

Rechly: "Boy, you speak to me, tell me no! Do you know who I am?" Rechly temporarily gets up in Dan's face shouting at him for answering back and then realises he speaks his language. "Wait a minute, you speak to me! Do you understand what I'm saying to you boy, or do you just know random words?"

Dan: "I know what you wanted to do to my friend."

Rechly: "Take the others away, and leave me. This one stays with me; we need to have a little talk, don't we boy."

Lilechem Clearing

Back in the forest the clearing to Lilechem is only moments away when Christian and Maddox are once again surrounded.

Leychrian: "Sorry but we can't let you go telling your friends about what we've done with your boys now can we?"

Maddox: "They're alive?"

Leychrian: "Not for long" he sniggers.

Maddox: "Are you strong enough to fight?" He asks Christian.

Christian: "Always" he says, getting off the griffin in mild discomfort.

Leychrian: "Rechly didn't say anything about bringing them back alive," his eyes light up, "it's dinner time."

The two brave Jenoans stand back to back and draw their swords. They begin slashing and gashing their way through the attacking mob, being bitten, scratched and beaten. After killing or wounding about fifteen Leychrians, they hear a trumpet sound from a nearby patrol coming to their rescue. A scout waiting for their arrival has spotted them and sounded the alarm. The Leychrians begin to scatter back to their master's castle. A Jenoan on a griffin rides up to them, as his other soldiers chase away the fleeing Leychrians - creatures covered with short hair all over their bodies, who can walk on their two back legs like the Jenoans, or on all fours.

Maverick: "Are you alright?"

Christian: "I've had better days. You look familiar, do we know you?"

Maverick: "My name is Maverick, come let's get you back to Lilechem, and we can take care of your wound there. Is this all that's left of you?"

Maddox: "No, our children, Rechly has them. We must go rescue them."

Maverick: "It will be dark shortly; we need to get you back before the shadow beasts attack. Rechly won't kill them; he can use them as bait for bigger food or sell them off as slaves. He doesn't eat children unless they have no food." They begin riding off with Maverick.

Rechly's Dungeon

In the dark, damp depths of Rechly's castle, the nine boys await their fate.

James: "Do you think we'll get out of here?"

Graeme: "Yes, I have no doubt."

James: “How can you be so sure?”

Graeme: “I never said we’d get out alive, just out of here and onto a dinner plate I should guess.”

Corey: “That’s comforting.”

Ben: “Did you see though, Dan had a Hader? Why would he have a Hader, Mal?”

Mal: “I don’t think Dan is from a world belonging to our system; he knows hardly anything about any of the planets I’ve been talking about and I’ve never come across a world called Earth before. Alemap must have given it to him so he can understand us, which sounds all too familiar.”

Jordan: “What do you mean?”

Mal: “Remember when our parents used to tell us about the Legendary Phoenix?”

Jordan: “Well, he’s no legend, never mind anything to do with a Phoenix.”

Jake: “I could beat him in a sword fight with my eyes closed.” He stood by the door and listened out for any signs of life, while the others all spread out in their cell looking for an escape route.

Matthew: “I know he isn’t from around these parts, but there could be any number of reasons why he’s here.”

Ryan: “Yes, because Shonrar is the most popular tourist destination in this part of the galaxy.”

Mal: “I know, but it’s all this talk about horses, and the clothes he wears. What planet round here has horses?”

Ben: “I know and they ride them, how crazy is that? Didn’t he say he’s human or something?”

Corey: "Hold on, if he is the Legendary Phoenix in our generation, then we are his council, nine of us, that's right isn't it?"

Graeme: "In which case we're going to get out of this alive."

James: "What's the rhyme they used to tell?" Between them they remember, "When tragedy strikes on boys of nine, from castles black and through dangerous times. A council to the Phoenix be, in times of need till in service are three."

Jordan: "What's the rest of it?"

Jake: "I don't suppose it matters now, your theory is going to be put to the test; someone's coming."

Three Leychrian guards come to the dungeon door, one remains by it while the other two bring masses of food in for them and then leave.

Matthew: "What's this?"

Ryan: "Do you think it's poisoned?"

Jordan: "I doubt it. If it's poisoned and we eat it, then they eat us, they'll be poisoned too."

Ryan: "What if the poison doesn't affect them?"

Jake: "I'm so hungry."

Matthew: "Me too." The boys gather around the food while the guard watches them from outside the open door.

Ben: "What are we going to do?"

Corey: "I'll eat some, then give it an hour or so and if I die then…"

Dan: "You can all eat, it's not poisoned." He said being led into the cell.

Mal: "Dan!" The door was closed and locked behind him.

Graeme: "What happened?"

James: "Are you alright?"

Jake: "Are you sure we can eat it?"

Dan: "Yes, tuck in." They begin ravenously munching their way through the food.

Jordan: "So what happened with Rechly?" he asked with his mouth full.

Dan: "He's keeping us here till morning, then he's going to sell you off as slaves." They paused in their eating.

Matthew: "Us, not you?"

Dan: "No, he wants to keep me as insurance in case Lilechem does send guards, or until he has a boss who needs a new slave that can understand multiple languages. I think he said he's going to hide the Hader from sight somehow, like it is a natural talent I have or something."

Ryan: "So we need to escape before morning then?"

Matthew: "I don't get it, why morning? Rechly and his men can go out anytime without fear of the shadow beings."

Dan: "I think he doesn't want them claiming us for themselves. Anyway, I heard something else interesting…he was trying to talk in secret with his brother, you know the one from before?"

Mal: "Teburnt?"

Dan: "Yeah, I think that was his name. Anyway, they were too far away for me to hear what they were talking about to begin with, but when Teburnt upset Rechly because he didn't capture your Dads..."

Corey: "They're still alive?"

Ryan: "That means they must have made it to Lilechem."

Corey: "Which means we'll be getting rescued." He said in a loud excited voice.

Mal: "Sssshhh, the guards might hear you."

Corey: "But they don't speak Jenoan, do they?"

Dan: "Well, it sounds like there are a lot of humans, sorry, Jenoans passing through here for slavery or as meals, so it comes to reason that they might have at least one thing able to understand us. Anyway, back to the point. I overheard them talking about a package they have got for their boss. Something priceless that would guarantee them favour with whomever. They didn't mention a name, but they sounded quite important and not very patient."

James: "Milo?"

Dan: "Who's Milo?"

Ben: "He's someone who has been exiled to the mountains in the west because of fear of what he will do. He used to be our healer before Alemap, but after what happened..."

Dan: "Why, what happened?"

Matthew: "My Dad said his son was killed in a tragic accident and he blames the Shonrar leaders for not taking care of his boy."

Ryan: "He was our age, a bit quiet, but nice enough."

Dan: "How did he die?"

Jake: "Wasn't he stabbed by an enemy?"

Jordan: "No, he drowned in the oasis." Turning to Dan, "the oasis is a big lake in the Shonrar woods."

Corey: "No, he got eaten by Leychrians, didn't he?"

Mal: "The point is, he's dead, and it wasn't from natural causes."

Dan: "Did they really have to exile him though?"

Graeme: "He was plotting to kill Lord Stephen. With him gone, he would be next in line to rule Shonrar."

James: "He could also be the one who killed Lord Stephen's father as revenge."

Dan: "He must be lonely up on that mountain by himself."

Ben: "I doubt he is lonely. He'll have all the shadow beings helping him get revenge. They're not from these parts, but he got them to help us once before when we were attacked by a tribe from over the Sandy Mountains wishing to claim Shonrar as their own."

Milo's Cave

Milo is impatiently waiting for the remains of his dead son. The closer to dark it gets, the more anxious he gets that the Jenoans have taken them. Then once the sun dips behind his mountain, the shadow being comes back to him with a gift.

Shadow: "Your Master wishes you to have this gift and to remember who made it possible."

Milo: "Do you have all the bones?"

Shadow: "All that were there. The Yashel is a rare artefact and you should be thankful for the use of it."

Milo:	"Yes, I am. Now leave me so I can do what I need to do."
Shadow:	"Very well, but remember Rechly."
Milo:	"I will, now leave!" He yells. The shadow being departs and heads for Rechly's castle.

For a moment, Milo stands looking at the remains of his one and only son. "Don't worry; we will avenge your death together. With the Yashel I can bring you back. You won't be the same as you were, but maybe we can make you even better. It's a dangerous process but I need to bring you back. You have so much to live for and I have great plans for you." He starts extracting the soul from the bones of his son and placing it into the Yashel. "Now I have your soul in the Yashel, it won't be long before I can bring you back to me. I need you to do something for me though. Go to Rechly's domain, find the container similar to the Yashel and then I can steal it and use it to help sustain you in a physical form. I will guide you from here. We shall be reunited soon, I promise." The spirit of his son flies out of the Yashel, through the night towards Rechly's kingdom. Milo places his hands on the Yashel and is able to see what his son sees and guide him.

Leychr

Escape Plan

Dan: "So how are we going to get out of here?"

Graeme: "Any suggestions?"

James: "Well, if someone distracts the guards while we sneak out of the door and find a way out of here, then we'll come back for you or get help first."

Dan: "So if you six distract the guard, we'll sneak out. They don't look intelligent enough to remember how many were in here to begin with anyway." Four of the boys, including Dan, hide behind the door while the other six create a distraction. Sure enough, the big slow guard with a muzzle round his mouth came in and went over to where the boys were. The other four slipped out the door and headed down the corridor.

Once clear, the boys in the cell behaved and stood in full view of the door. The creature left the room and locked it up again. He looked at a notice on the wall and then re-entered the room, blocking the door with his enormous body. He started pointing at the boys one by one who were relatively in a line.

Ben: "He's counting us."

Mal: "Come together, all stand in a line."

Ryan: "But he'll notice then there aren't enough of us."

Mal: "Not necessarily, watch this." Mal was standing at the right hand side of the line where the creature began counting from. He watched him count the boy next to him and then when he got to the third boy in, he ducked behind and ran to the end of the line. He indicated to the other boys when to do the same. Unfortunately, one of the boys got carried away and went to the end of the line, bringing the guard's count to eleven. The guard slowly dragged his body out the door, checked the list and returned to the room and began counting again from the left. They tried the sequence again.

Having more luck, the other four boys manage to move around the kingdom more easily. They can hear noises coming from the hall they were first in. As they approach it quietly, they notice the Leychrians celebrating, so they continue searching the castle. After a while they find a possible escape.

James: "We should go back and tell the others."

Graeme: "How are we going to get the others out?"

Dan: "There was just a bolt on the door, right?"

Corey: "Yes."

Dan: "Well, if we throw a stone past the guard. He'll go and investigate. Then if we move the bolt back and let everyone out, we could be out of there before he comes back."

Corey: "Let's do it." They head back, avoiding the dining area towards the dungeon. On the way, Dan looks out of a window and sees a light. He then sees Rechly cover the light with a cloth.

James: "It's Rechly, what's he doing?"

Dan: "I don't know but he's heading back this way. Hurry, hide." Rechly passes straight by them, running on all fours, heading to the dining area.

Graeme: "What do you think is in there?"

Dan: "I don't know, but I'm going to find out. Go ahead with the plan and meet me in that room, and don't be long, he might come back." The three boys head off to the cell, while Dan goes to investigate the light. From outside the door he cannot see the spirit entering the room from the window.

Dining Area

Rechly: "Go and do your safety check on the castle now, then you can enjoy yourself."

Teburnt: "OK" he says, grudgingly.

Rechly: "Oh and bring us back a boy for dessert. I think we've earned it, but only one. Pick the fattest one there is." The Leychrians cheer. "Anyone but the boy with the Hader. I want him for something special."

The Chamber

Dan finds the door to the room is unlocked. He is ecstatic when he finds their weapons are in the room. He attaches the knife back to his belt, leaves the door slightly ajar and heads for the light, glowing underneath the cloth. As he goes to remove it he doesn't notice the spirit on the ceiling, but does hear footsteps coming towards the door.

The Cell

Things don't exactly go to plan for the three returning boys. The plan runs on course, until the bolt on the door makes a loud squeak, which makes the guard run right back to their cell. They manage to open the door and run in, with the guard hot on their tails. The boys are pulled aside by Mal and the others. The guard runs into the middle of the cell and the boys run out, shutting and bolting the door behind them.

Teburnt enters the room where Dan is.

Teburnt: "Well, well, what do we have here?"

Dan: "Don't you come near me or, or…"

Teburnt: "Or what?"

Dan: "I'll scream?"

Teburnt: "Go ahead." Teburnt starts running towards him and Dan picks up the shining object to throw at him. Teburnt stops dead in his tracks. The cover falls off exposing the light, the light dims and they can see it is a jar.

Teburnt: "What are you doing with that? Put it down. Let's talk about this."

Dan: "What is there to talk about? You're about to kill me." Teburnt edges closer to Dan. "Stay where you are."

Teburnt: "No, I'm not, don't be silly. Just put the jar down."

Dan: "Or what?" he raises the jar above his head.

Teburnt: "No, no, Rechly will kill me."

Dan: "Move away, that's it round there." Dan keeps the jar above his head and backs towards the door. The spirit follows the jar towards the door. Teburnt notices it and it hides behind a pillar.

The rest of the boys get to the chamber.

Dan: "Quick, take your weapons and a sword each; Mal get an extra one for me too."

Teburnt: "Where are you going with that?" Dan checks everyone is out of the room. He notices Teburnt glancing at the ceiling and then sees the spirit floating around above him. Teburnt takes this opportunity to attack.

Dan: "You want it, it's yours!" He hurls it across the room. He is just about to leave when he notices the spirit and Teburnt trying to stop it from smashing. It hits the floor and shatters. The ray of light from inside the jar fills the room. For a moment Dan and Teburnt are stunned and feel slightly dizzy but the effects soon wear off and Dan escapes the room, locking Teburnt in. He looks at the broken jar, cries out in despair and leaves through another exit at the far end of the room, concealed by a cloth, which he rips from the wall.

Milo

The same cries can be heard from Milo who is watching everything from the point of view of his son's spirit. He tells him to return to the cave.

Rechly

Rechly wonders where his brother is and goes to investigate. He heads down to the dungeon first where he sees the creature trapped inside. He undoes the bolted door and tells the guard to come out. "Get out of there. It's about time I got rid of you once and for all" he mutters. The guard, who has been trying to escape, doesn't realise the door is unlocked and runs into it, knocking it down. Rechly gets trapped underneath. "OK maybe not dispose of you! Get off of me."

The Escape

The boys rush for the exit, but Teburnt blocks them off.

Teburnt: "Where do you think you're going?" he asks, his teeth clenched. They run into the nearest room locking the door behind them.

Dan: "Everyone spread out, draw your swords and get ready to fight." Teburnt bangs on the door and it shakes on its hinges. After a few seconds it all goes silent. "Try that other door at the back."

Mal: "Where?"

Dan: "Look you can just see it behind that curtain."

James: "It's locked from the other side."

Corey: "We're trapped."

Dan: "It's all gone quiet out there. Has he gone?" They slowly walk towards the door when the door bursts open behind them and in run Christian and Maddox, just in time to see Teburnt knock down the front door.

Though worried, he is obviously outnumbered; he goes for Dan, knocking down a few of the other boys along the way. Maddox pushes Dan out of the way and lunges at Teburnt with his sword. Dan falls to the ground and crawls under a nearby table to avoid Teburnt's attempts to get to him. Meanwhile, Christian starts leading the other boys, except Mal, who is trapped between the broken down front door and the fighting. After a few more moments of intense fighting, Teburnt falls to the ground with Maddox's sword appearing to stick out of his chest. It is actually thrust between his arm and chest, but he is concealing the fact he isn't hurt and pretends to be dead. Mal runs past him, slides under the table and helps Dan to move, finding that he has been deeply wounded in the leg.

Mal: "What's wrong with your leg?" he asks looking disgusted.

Dan: "I got injured" he says, as they try to get out from under the table.

Mal: "I know, but what's that red stuff coming out of your wound?"

Dan: "Blood" he says, confused.

Mal: "Blood? But it's red!" he proclaims, as though he's never seen it before.

As they reach the end of the table, Maddox's hands reach down to pull them out. Teburnt appears behind him and stabs him in the back with his own sword. Dan reaches out to grab Maddox's hand, but he falls forward, blood spilling from his mouth as he is pulled away from the table. Dan falls backwards with Maddox's necklace in his hand. Dan and Mal scramble from under the table. They look on at Maddox shouting at them to run away, as Teburnt looks the boys in the eyes and grins with a proud satisfaction and then bites a large chunk out of Maddox's neck, rendering him dead. Mal, in shock, and Dan, in pain from his leg, scramble through the back door. Locking it they partly run down to the gesturing arms of Christian, who is encouraging them to hurry. As they are running, they hear a shrieking noise. They look back to see if Teburnt has got through the door but it is still closed. They then turn to the window, realising the noises are coming from the chamber, where Rechly is furiously angry. His possessions have been destroyed and he is panicking that he won't be able to fulfil his transaction to his boss.

Revenge

As Dan and Mal reach the bottom of the tunnel, which leads out into a garden exit to the kingdom, there are Lilechem soldiers armed and riding on griffins. Christian pats them on the shoulder and smiles that they are out of the castle and alive. Noticing the look of pain and despair on their faces, he looks back up the tunnel and asks where Maddox is.

Dan: "He's not coming."

Christian: "Where is he?"

Dan: "Dead!"

Christian: "What? Are you sure?"

Dan: "Teburnt ripped out his throat, I'm sure. He's on our heels. He'll be here anytime now, we need to leave." Christian stands frozen at the thought of his oldest friend dead. "Christian, we need to leave now." Dan demanded. Christian draws his sword. "No, he won't get away with this. Go to the griffins, NOW."

The boys set off towards the soldiers where Maverick is beckoning them on. He goes back towards the griffins to get them ready to go.

Dan: "Was it just me or was your Dad's blood orange?" Mal was too upset to know what he was talking about and just blankly carried on. They hurry as best they can, hearing Christian's shouts of emotional pain as he sees the beast who killed Maddox running on all fours towards him, blood dripping from it's mouth and an evil glint in it's eyes. Mal looks back over his shoulder and then looks at Dan.

Dan: "No, you can't go back, he'll kill you." As he is saying it, Teburnt leaps at Christian knocking him to the ground in the garden outside the castle.

"I'm going." Mal says. Dan grabs him by the arm, but Mal easily pulls away dragging him to the ground. Teburnt knocks Christian over a nearby wall as he gets to his feet and turns towards Dan and Mal, who is now running towards him with the same look as Christian. As Teburnt gets near Mal, he jumps straight over the top of him, his focus only on Dan. With Teburnt running at him, Dan begins to back off. He is still on the floor and starts crawling backwards. Teburnt leaps on top of him, drooling, "I'm going to enjoy this."

Mal turns around and now runs back to Dan, with his sword drawn. In front of him, Teburnt is sideways on, ready to show Mal his next kill. About to sink his teeth into Dan, out of the corner of his eye Teburnt sees the glint of Mal's sword in the moonlight. He turns his head to the side and raises an arm to attack Mal. Dan, still squirming under him, sees what he is about to do, reaches for the dagger in his belt and plunges it into Teburnt's heart. Teburnt's head drops down towards Dan. Christian, now back on his feet, throws a knife toward Teburnt, who is dead from Dan's dagger. Meanwhile Mal's blade chops off Teburnt's head and Christian's knife sends the decapitated body of the beast onto the floor a few feet from Dan, who is caught by the edge of Mal's blade. Dan looks at the remains of Teburnt and sees green blood seeping onto the ground around him. He looks to Mal for comfort.

Mal: "What is it?" Dan turns the other way and throws up on the ground. Christian grabs the boys and drags them off to the griffins and the soldiers who are awaiting an immediate departure, but first kicks Teburnt's head into the foliage.

Rechly, now with his soldiers, enters the room with a dead Maddox, his blood spreading across the floor, and smiles at his brother's handy work. He notices the far door has also been knocked down. He goes through the first, and then second door at top speed, worrying about his brother, as the rest begin to tuck into the leftovers of Maddox. He bounds down the corridor to the rear gardens of the castle. He gets to the bottom and looks to the right to see the broken wall Teburnt had thrown Christian through. He immediately leaps over it, but seeing nothing, he looks back in the opposite direction to see a lifeless corpse. Fearing the worst, he goes to it. Even without the head, he knows it is Teburnt. He cries out to the moon, snarls and runs round the garden area to try find the culprits.

Mal is riding in a carriage with Dan and trying to wrap up the wound he inflicted on him. Dan groans in pain.

Mal: "I'm so sorry, I didn't mean to stab you. I got him though," he said with a mixture of hate and pleasure in his eyes.

Dan: "It's alright" even though Dan had killed Teburnt, it had all happened so fast he didn't know which blade had finished him off. "Your father would have been proud."

Mal: "Do you still have it?"

Dan: "Here." Dan pulls Mal's father's necklace out of his pocket and passes it to him, but passes out from the pain before Mal gets it.

Mal: "Christian, we've got to get him some medical help fast." They ride to Lilechem as fast as possible.

Tasks & Training

Alemap's Home

Dan starts to come round to the sun shining in his eyes and the sound of running water again. He is in Alemap's home. Alemap is in the room with him but she doesn't notice him stirring on the couch. She is cleaning in the room and humming a song in which she mentions two Phosian towns Ebilay and Ebaliy.

Dan: "Alemap, what am I doing here?"

Alemap: "Dan! At last! I was wondering when you would come to."

Dan: "How did I get here? I thought we were on our way to Lilechem."

Alemap: "You were. You went there after the attack on Leychr. You had medical treatment there until it was safe to move you and then you were brought back here."

Dan: "How long have I been out of it?"

Alemap: "Just a couple of days."

Dan: "A couple of days of my life lost, kinda scary when you think about it." He sits up. "What are Ebilay and Ebaliy?"

Alemap: "They are towns that are to the south of us, where did you hear those names?"

Dan: "You were singing them a minute ago when I woke up."

Alemap: "Yes, I suppose I was. Anyway, you sit there and I'll get you something to eat. You must be starving."

Dan: "That would be great, thanks. I am now you mention it."

Alemap goes to prepare something for him and makes contact with someone, telling them Dan has woken up and to get here fast. Without waiting for a reply she cuts communication and continues making Dan's food.

Alemap: "So now you're awake, I think it's time we had that chat."

Dan: "What about?"

Alemap: "Well, about you and why you're really here."

Dan: "Oh, OK then."

Alemap: "Along time ago…"

Dan: "…In a far off kingdom…"

Alemap: "Sorry?"

Dan: "Never mind, it doesn't matter, carry on."

Alemap: "Along time ago, there was a prophecy about someone who would come to Phosia to help us battle against the raging war here. Well actually, we didn't know at the time it would happen on Phosia. I think every planet in the universe thought it could be them, but when we were contacted by the MPC Superiors about your arrival we knew it was Phosia."

Dan: "War, you don't seem to be at war."

Alemap: "Not at the moment, but things have been tense

to say the least between some of the races of Phosia and we could be invaded from beings beyond our lands at anytime."

Dan: "So why am I here?"

Alemap: "The prophecy talks about one who will come from the stars in a blaze of glory and shall live amongst us, protecting us from attack. There's no mistaking that it's you. Anyway, you have to prove yourself worthy of your destiny by fulfilling three tasks that were decreed at the time of the prophecy. Once you have completed these tasks, we will be able to use a weapon to save not only us but countless others. However, only you can unlock the power of the weapon in order to save us."

Dan: "What are these tasks I am supposed to do?"

Alemap: "Well, one of them you've already completed."

Dan: "I have when?"

Alemap: "On your visit to Leychr. There was an item that was to be given to a source of evil. They could have used it to find the weapon for his or herself; it was a jar with glowing light, I take it. I'm sure that they will not give up trying to find another way to get the weapon for themselves though. The forces of evil run rife through this and many other worlds and the force that helps them is powerful, politically at least. There are many cases where things that have happened would not be possible without intervention by well connected beings."

Dan: "Erm, I have to say I accidentally broke it. Well, not accidentally. I used it as a distraction to escape. I'm sorry if you needed it."

Alemap: "No, don't be sorry, that's fine. As long as we have you, we should be all right. If the item was destroyed then at least whomever Rechly was to give it to can't use it against us."

Dan: "Can't you find out from Rechly who he's working for?"

Alemap: "No, not really. Yes, I'm sure we could find out whom he is to give the item to, but I believe that it will pass through many hands before getting to the being or group that organised everything. What's wrong?" Dan was looking a bit peaky.

Dan: "I've just remembered seeing Maddox being killed and Teburnt. They had different colours of blood! Maddox was orange…" she nodded "…and Teburnt's was green."

Alemap: "Yes, well don't the species on Earth have different coloured blood?"

Dan: "I don't think so."

Alemap: "Well don't forget, anything you can't explain is probably the fact we come from two different worlds. If there's anything you don't understand, you can always come and ask me. I'm happy to try to get us both to understand each others cultures, etc."

Dan: "So that was my first task then?"

Alemap: "Well, actually that wasn't really to do with the task, we found out about the item through… well you don't really want to know how we found it out." Alemap remembers seeing a Leychrian being tortured via her Hader. "The task part was to rescue your peers and bring down an influential member of our enemies camp, i.e. Teburnt. He was Rechly's brother and well respected. They ruled Leychr together. Rechly, being the eldest, was in command but he often made decisions based on Teburnt's point of view."

Dan: "Wow, I don't know what to say."

Alemap: "To tell you the truth, we didn't see how you were going to pull this off. It just shows you are the 'Chosen One'."

Dan: "So what are the other two tasks?"

Alemap: "Well, one is that you must retrieve something from somewhere by yourself, without the help of anyone else."

Dan: "That sounds a bit vague."

Alemap: "Well, the task is to be set by Lord Stephen or whoever is in charge at the time of alignment."

Dan: "What and when is that?"

Alemap: "You'll find out in good time."

Dan: "And the last task?"

Alemap: "Well the last…" she shakes her head "…I mean the third task is to get to the weapon."

Dan: "That's it?"

Alemap: "Well, you have to locate it first and then get to it. Then there will be the actual operation of it, but we should concentrate on the second task now."

Dan: "Can't you tell me where it is, the weapon?"

Alemap: "I don't know, but you do, or you will when the time is right."

Dan: "Well that sounds simpler."

Alemap: "In theory yes."

Dan: "So why me, what did I do to deserve this?"

Alemap: "You were chosen by higher beings that could foretell your destiny and knew you would be the one strong enough to complete the tasks and, for lack of a better term, win the prize."

There is a knock at the door. "We will talk later, for now there is someone here to see you. Go on, you get it." Dan walks over to the door. When he opens it he doesn't recognise who it is. Alemap sits down with a smile on her face. "Hello, can I help you?" Alemap turns around. The being at the door pulls out a sharp weapon to attack Dan. He runs back into the room towards where Alemap was sitting, but she has disappeared. The being knocks Dan to the ground and is about to stab him when Mal appears behind him and plunges his dagger into his back. The being falls to the ground. Mal has a flashback to his father dying in the same way, but shakes it off.

Mal: "There I am saving you again."

Dan: "At least you didn't stab me in the process this time." Alemap came out from another room with a sword. She notices the being has been dealt with. "Mal, nice to see you."

Mal: "Hi, is it alright if we go to training now?" Mal helps Dan to his feet. Christian appears in the open doorway.

Christian: "That sounds like a good idea to me. Run along you two I'll be there in a moment." The boys leave, talking about Dan's scars. "So how is he, will he be OK for training?"

Alemap: "He seems alright, but I'd take it easy on him for a few days just in case. Let me know if he has any problems."

Christian: "Of course."

Alemap: "That attack didn't seem to faze either of them very much."

Christian: "After what they've just been through on their excursion to Leychr, one assassin isn't going to be much to them. So how are you? Coping with being his mentor?"

Alemap: "It's a big responsibility. One I'm not sure if I'm ready for. I'm worried now that he won't make it to his next task. Obviously someone has informed the evil behind this, that Dan is the 'Chosen One'. How can I protect him against an unlimited number of attacks from who knows what beings?"

Christian: "You leave protecting him to me, we don't know who the being was after. I will have the body removed for you and try to find out some information. Dan and the rest of the boys will have training, just like me and…" he stops and lowers his head.

Alemap: "If you need to talk about anything, let me know. It must be a hard time for you too, especially now the full burden of training is with you and not shared with Maddox."

Christian: "As long as I train these boys up to the best of my knowledge, I should be fine. That's the best way I can avenge his death now. Besides, the other fathers help me out where they can, but this is my job, they have their own responsibilities."

Alemap: "Well, if you change your mind about talking you know where to find me."

Christian: "Thank you." Lord Stephen arrives to check how Dan is. Alemap welcomes him in and the three of them sit down for a chat.

Alemap: "Anyway, I shall be getting to see how well you are doing with your training of the boys when they compete as Falcons at the festival."

Christian: "Ah yes, the Phosian mid summer festival. It will be interesting to see how Dan competes against girls."

Lord Stephen: "What do you mean?"

Christian: "Well so far the only girl he's seen is… well you." He said looking at Alemap.

Alemap: "There are girls in the village."

Christian: "Yes, but he trains in an all boy group, he is educated by you and when he's in the village with the boys he tends to hang out with the boys. Not that he's had much time to relax since he's been here."

Lord Stephen: "I see what you mean. Well, maybe it's the same where he comes from. We really should do more research into his planet's history and teach him some of their cultures too for when he returns to his home planet."

Christian: "If he returns."

Alemap: "That's a very negative view of things." She says scornfully.

Christian: "It is, but we have to face facts. Dan may not return home. He has a lot of obstacles to overcome before he leaves, which I don't think we could achieve if they were ours. If it wasn't for the fact that he is prophesied to achieve the impossible then I wouldn't believe it myself."

Alemap: "And the fact that he has completed the first of the three." She stated proudly, as a mother would of her child.

Christian: "Yes, that too."

Alemap: "So how much do you think I should tell him? Should I just come out with it and tell him all the prophecies we believe are connected to him or just see what happens?"

Lord Stephen: "Don't tell him anymore than he needs to know. We have found many prophecies and they aren't all about Dan. We have to be certain they are about him. There are ones mentioning someone's death. We don't want to be telling him about that if it isn't him. I have my sources working on it."

Christian: "What about the other thing?"

Lord Stephen: "What other thing?"

Christian: "You know about how he got here."

Lord Stephen: "Oh yes. Well, that's quite a delicate situation; we'll let Alemap tell him when she feels he is ready to know."

Alemap: "What, why me?"

Lord Stephen: "Because you are his guardian. He picked you himself."

Alemap: "I wouldn't know what to say. He's so innocent."

Christian: "Not anymore he's not. He's a killer."

Alemap: "Look, what he did he didn't mean to do."

Lord Stephen: "It was self defence."

Alemap: "What are you talking about, oh when he killed Rechly's brother?"

Lord Stephen: "That's another thing. With Teburnt gone do you think Rechly will return to the land he and his hoard came from?"

Christian: "No I doubt it. They like it here but there may be a struggle to fill Teburnt's place. I think Rechly will have his hands full for a while, making sure he isn't overthrown. I don't think we have anything to worry about as far as him planning an attack is concerned."

Lord Stephen: "Well Alemap, I leave Dan's well-being in your capable hands and his training in yours, Christian. Between us we can hopefully save Shonrar from devastation and keep him alive in the process. I'll be off now. I shall see you both at the festival-planning meeting tomorrow I take it? How are we fairing up this year?"

Christian: "Yes, we're looking fine and with the 'Chosen One' on our team we should have no problem."

Alemap: "Yes, but he's not the 'Chosen One' yet. He's just an ordinary boy, albeit that he is from another planet. Plus he's only just arrived, do you think it's right we enter him in the festival?"

Christian: "Well, we did enter ten boys into the competition and Dan makes the tenth. We can't help that one... dropped out." He looks at his Hader. "I must be off now. Don't want to be late to training do I?"

Lord Stephen: "One thing before we go, can we not refer to him as the 'Chosen One' or anything anymore. After all, his presence here is supposed to be a secret to the outside world."

Alemap: "OK then, see you soon." They say their goodbyes and Christian leaves with Lord Stephen. Alemap goes straight over to a computer screen and contacts a colleague of hers. "Laup? Yes, I've just remembered something very important. Human blood is red; we need to order Tamtun and lots of it. Get me some in a dissolvable form so I can put it in his drink, thank you." She ends communication.

Dan's Tour Of Shonrar

Since his arrival was so chaotic, Christian decides Dan should have a tour of Shonrar from his fellow Falcons. They start off by taking him to the town centre where they have market stalls and plenty of Jenoans and other species walking around. It is an experience for Dan, not only seeing all the non-human looking creatures, but Shonrar itself is a real eye opener compared to what he is used to on Earth. The town centre is in between the hills of Shonrar and they are all grouped quite closely together. Standing at the top of a hill, Dan can see down into the town centre. As he looks ahead, he can see the Great Hall in the distance, behind Shonrar's tower and behind him is the waterfall where Alemap resides and some cottages leading around the mountainside to the stables.

Dan: "It's so beautiful."

Mal: "It is, isn't it?" Dan notices lots of structures erected on the hills around and asks Mal what they are for. "Well, Shonrar is very environmentally conscious after the destruction of a few planets from pollution and it uses these structures to capture sunlight and turn it into energy."

Corey: "The light from the sun is used to heat water and to provide electricity for all these homes" he said gesturing to the hills around them. Dan looked around "what homes, I don't see any houses?"

Jake: "You're standing on them now." Dan looks down.

Graeme: "The houses are underground. If you look down there, you'll see a door and some windows at the bottom of the hill." Dan looked and was happily surprised to see a Jenoan coming out of their home and heading towards the town centre.

Dan: "How cool is that! So you have all your power provided through the sun then?"

Jordan: "No, we use wind and hydro electricity too."

Matthew: "They have generators on Spencer Island that provide energy from the tide going in and out."

Dan: "Where's Spencer Island?"

Ryan: "Erm… they also use tidal energy in Bela… I mean Ebilay and Ebaliy, they're on the beach," he said pointing to the cliff wall facing the back of Shonrar.

Ben: "If you look up there, at the top you might see some of the turbines."

Dan: "So every where's got some form of renewable energy source?"

Mal: "Yep, pretty much. They have some in Leychr too but I don't think the Leychrians would know how to use it, besides they have fur coats so they won't need heat."

Dan: "They had lights on in the tower and the dungeon though, when we were there."

Jordan: "Some of the systems would be on automatic and if they fail then they wouldn't know what to do to fix it."

Dan: "The tower? Is it similar to the one we have over there?" he asks, looking up at the structure.

Jake: "Yes, they have one in each of the large cities; Leychr, Shonrar and Lilechem."

Ryan: "They used them to communicate with each other in the past."

Dan: "How?"

Mal: "All sorts of ways, birds to fly in between, lights in the night, etc."

Dan: "Our worlds aren't that much different after all; there are so many similarities." Dan asks the boys where they live and they each in turn point out the area in which they dwell. Some lived in the cottages, some in the submerged housing and others, like Mal in the complex built into the waterfall and Sandy Mountains.

The Phosian Mid-summer Festival

Shonrar Heats

As the boys look forward to their participation as Shonrar Falcons, their aim is to represent Shonrar in the next competition, which puts two groups from Shonrar against challengers from the nearby cities of Lilechem, Ebilay and Ebaliy. For the heats, only family are allowed to watch along with the city officials, including Lord Stephen, who leads the proceedings. Seats for the spectators have been provided in the form of the griffin's haystacks to one side of the courtyard. The challengers each try their best in the four categories of hand-to-hand combat, a race to the Shonrar Lake and back, archery and fencing. Two prestigious prizes are also given to one challenger from each group for their overall performance, and one to the group who performs best as a team. This last award is given after a game of dodge ball where two teams fight on the same side against another two. All the points awarded are by the spectators, but families of the Falcons only vote for those on the other teams and so on.

Dan and the other boys have just finished a training session and have a few hours to kill before they have to be back for the heats. They decide to go into town. As they are walking around the town they are spotted by a group of girls who begin to stare and giggle at them. Corey gets annoyed with them thinking they are making fun of them. He starts to walk towards them when James tells Jordan to bring him back. Jordan goes after him and grabs him by the arm. Corey turns around to see Jordan and his big build and forgets the insult he was about to hurl.

Corey: "What do you want fat… erm… Jordan."

Jordan: "James wants you."

Corey: "One minute, I just…"

Jordan: "No now" he insisted.

Corey: "OK, I'm coming." They went back over to the other boys. "What is it James."

James: "Don't you know who those girls are?"

Corey: "Should I?"

James: "They're our competition."

Corey: "So."

Ryan: "What he's trying to say is that they want to distract you from the competition later."

Matthew: "Oh yeah, my Dad was telling me about this one group of girls who got their friends who weren't competing to keep a whole team of boys distracted until it was too late for them to qualify."

Ben: "That seems a bit extreme for some heats."

Matthew: "No, it was at the festival but they could be starting earlier this time. If we don't qualify in the heats we can't compete in the festival can we?"

Ryan: "Why don't we send Graeme over? He's the ladies man."

Graeme: "What?"

Corey: "Since when?" Ryan winked to Corey. "Oh yeah, of course you are. You seem to get all the looks from the girls normally."

Graeme: "I do?"

Ryan: "Yeah, now you go over and find out what they want and then come back. Just don't be going off anywhere with them, we have to leave soon."

Graeme: "OK then, here I go." Graeme was a bit dubious about why he had been chosen to go and talk to the young girls, given that the others normally teased him for his spotty complexion. The other boys waited for a few minutes and smiled at the girl's coy glances while Graeme talked to them. When he returned they were all eager to know what had been said.

Graeme: "Right then, let's go."

Mal: "What did they say?"

Graeme: "They were really nice." He said with a smile on his face and walked off towards the courtyard.

Ryan: "So what did they want?" he asked as they all went after him?

Graeme: "Oh, you were right. They said they wanted us to meet at the other end of the city in half an hour."

Jordan: "And what did you say?"

Graeme: "I said we'd all meet them there." They sniggered and walked off together.

Ben: "But what if we're wrong and they actually do like us?" they all stopped in their tracks to ponder the possibility then looked at each other.

Falcons: "Na" they said, shaking their heads and continued on.

Heat One

When arriving in the courtyard the boys were quickly ushered to get ready for the heats. When it was their turn to come out, they walked on with their heads held high to take their places. When they were ready, they began to notice the girls from town ready and waiting in their positions for the first heat, the run to and from Shonrar Lake. The girls looked disappointed that their plan hadn't worked, but after a few looks in their direction they settled down and concentrated on the task at hand. They were determined not to let the Falcons gloat about winning as well.

Lord Stephen started the race by shooting an arrow at the large wooden gates that opened inwards, allowing access out of the city to the woods. He cheered on the contestants until they were out of sight and then sat back down in his chair next to Christian whilst awaiting their arrival back. Some of the spectators were watching the contest on the hologram provided, while others were watching it and checking out the other competitions on their Haders. Lord Stephen turned to Christian "So how is Dan doing then?"

Christian: "He's doing alright. He seems to fit in well with the other boys. They do tease him a bit over things he doesn't understand from the change of worlds, but seems to just laugh off the comments."

Lord Stephen: "And what about his training?"

Christian: "Well, he's OK. I've only worked with him for a few months and he has a lot of catching up to do compared to the others but he should be fine. He tries hard and does a few extra sessions with me to help him along."

Lord Stephen: "So he hasn't got any special abilities that are going to help us save Shonrar from destruction?"

Christian: "Not from what I have seen, but its early days. He is quite good at defending himself though, even from me. He has a real talent for deflecting blows like he knows they're coming before I do them."

When the runners began returning, the Falcons were not the first to return and as the day and competitions went on the Shonrar Falcons failed to make the top spot.

Christian: "Well done boys, I'm very proud of you."

Ben: "But we didn't win." He said sulking.

Lord Stephen: "No you didn't but you did very well. Winning isn't everything..."

Dan: "…it's the taking part." He said sarcastically.

Lord Stephen: "You're so right Dan, thank you." Dan smiled to himself realising they didn't know it was a saying back on Earth.

Christian: "Besides there's always next year and just because you didn't win doesn't mean we aren't going to throw you a party to celebrate."

Ben: "Celebrate what? The fact that we're losers."

Christian: "No the fact that you are all talented and brave enough to enter the competition in the first place."

Ben: "Well, we only did it because it looks good for College applications."

Lord Stephen: "What ever the reason, you've done it and we're proud of you."

Christian: "Of course, if you don't want a party…"

Ben: "I didn't say that."

Christian: "Right, let's go then your families are waiting outside to congratulate you."

The Festival

After lots of preparation for the big event, the eve of the festival had arrived. Lots of officials had arrived in Shonrar, most from other planets representing the MPC. They had their own accommodation erected in the form of a large tent able to accommodate twenty beings. This was usual for the dignitaries, as they went to each of the cities in turn as the festival was held there. The dignitaries were watching some of the contestants training in preparation for the next day's events.

Though the Falcons hadn't gotten into the finals against the other cities, the boys weren't too bothered. They had had their party the night before and there were plenty of other events going on in preparation for the big day. The boys were also relieved to know the girls from town hadn't made it into the final either.

They were all having a great day, laughing and messing around, when Dan suddenly turned around.

Mal: "What is it?"

Dan: "I don't know, but it isn't a good feeling." The boys had gone for a walk and were in the empty courtyard where the heats had taken place. Dan was facing the open gates. He started walking towards them when he saw a figure in the trees. Then another appeared. As he looked closer his mouth dropped to the floor. "Jordan, hold Mal back, everyone else slowly walk towards the gates and help me close them." Jordan restrained Mal without hesitation.

Mal: "Dan, what's going on?"

Dan: "Boozemises!" As the brave Falcons edged slowly for the gates Mal started to struggle as the image of his father appeared from the trees. The Boozemises began running for the city. Dan and the others managed to get the doors closed only seconds before they could get to them. All but Dan moved away from the door. Without turning around Dan said to Mal "Go and tell Christian, quickly." Mal did what he asked. Dan then backed away from the door where the

Boozemises were beating their fists.

Matthew: "That must have been so hard for Mal seeing the corpse of his father."

Dan: "It was. Is there any way to stop Boozemises?" he said listening to the noises on the other side.

James: "If you decapitate them, why?"

Dan: "Well, didn't I hear from the stories you've been telling me, that the person controlling this type of Boozemises could use the person's skills from the memories of when they were alive?"

Ryan: "Yes, why."

Dan: "Because I think Maddox is scaling the wall." No sooner had he said it, the others were also open mouthed as they looked at the walking corpse up above them. Before they could warn Dan it jumped down from the top of the gates and landed next to him. Dan was in shock and didn't know what to do. The corpse looked at the quivering boy for a second as though the old Maddox was in there, but suddenly his eyes changed and an evil smile came upon his face as he lunged for Dan and sunk his teeth into his shoulder. Dan screamed out in pain. After releasing the boy from his jaws the Boozemises threw him to the ground and looked hungrily at the other boys. He was about to go for his next victim when a sharp weapon came flying towards him and pinned him by the neck on the doors.

Christian had arrived with backup and rushed over to the boys. "Is anyone hurt?" He quickly surveyed the area and checked the other boys promptly for scars before rushing over to Dan who was holding his bleeding shoulder. Dan was lying at the feet of Maddox's former frame. As Christian got to Dan, he started scrambling towards him away from the doors. The corpse was wriggling around on the door trying to get to them.

Dan: "I thought once they were decapitated they stopped."

Christian: "They do" he replied getting to his feet. He could see the fear in the boy's eyes and knew straight away he would have to sort the Boozemises out to put them all at ease. Carefully trying to avoid injury, Christian pulled the weapon from the corpse's neck. It fell to the floor body first followed by the head but quickly disappeared into the floor.

Dan: "Is it gone, is it dead?"

Christian: "Yes, don't worry" He turned to the other leaders of Shonrar who were standing with their sons. Alemap ran over to Dan, and Christian's son Matthew ran to him. "Leaders of Shonrar, we must depart now for Lilechem."

Matthew: "Dad, don't go." He looked down at his son.

Christian: "I must. We have to get Dan some medicine from Lilechem quickly, else he will be turned into a Boozemises too."

Matthew: "Take me with you. I feel safer with you."

Christian: "No you must stay here with the rest of the boys. We may not be back for a while."

Alemap: "Don't worry Dan, everything will be alright" she said nursing him in her arms. "Christian and the others are going to get you some help."

Christian: "Go fetch the griffins" he said to the other leaders. "Matthew; watch over the other boys for me while I'm away. I'm counting on you."

Matthew: "Yes father, but what about the other Boozemises?"

Christian: "Don't worry they won't be able to get through the door. I doubt any of the others had talents the controller can use; not like Maddox's. Besides they sound to have gone now, listen." The banging on the doors had ceased. "It will take a lot of energy for the being controlling the Boozemises to do anything more now than keeping them alive and leading them in the right direction. They will probably be on automatic, killing anything in their path. The rest of the city should be safe. Go to the others now, I'll see you soon." Matthew walked back over to the other boys while Christian crouched down next to Alemap.

Christian: "We've been tracking down the remains of Maddox over the past few months in the fear this would happen. After we get Dan cured and some injections for us in case we get bitten, we will head out from Lilechem to check out a few of our sources. Can you take Mal back to his mother? He's with Lord Stephen now. He's quite shaken up, as you'd expect."

Alemap: "Of course I will. Look after him." She looked down at Dan "Christian will take you now. I will see you when you get back."

Dan: "Make sure Mal's alright for me. Unless he asks don't tell him about me. I don't want him to worry."

Alemap: "OK, I won't unless he brings it up." She helped Christian lift Dan onto a griffin and then stood well back with the others, watching as the Shonrar leaders opened the gates. They swiftly disposed of the Boozemises heading back into the woods before riding on to Lilechem.

Dan's Gut Feeling

They hadn't got far when Dan who was drifting in and out of consciousness on Christian's griffin suddenly sat up.

Dan: "Go back!" He demanded.

Christian: "Are you alright?"

Dan: "Go back, you have to go back."

Christian: "We have to get you to Lilechem and find the remains of Maddox and the others. If not they could keep coming back and you'll be one of them."

Dan: "Stop!" he screamed. Christian and the others stopped. Dan looked ahead towards Lilechem. "Send two on. There isn't anything there. Get them to bring back some medicine for those in Shonrar. They're going to need it." Dan was speaking with such conviction he almost seemed possessed.

Christian: "Are you sure about this?"

Dan: "You must trust me; do it, there isn't time to argue."

Christian: "OK. Julian. Simon, you go on ahead. The rest of us will return to Shonrar…"

Dan: "No, send everyone else back immediately." Christian looked at the others.

Christian: "Well you heard him. Go at full speed and report back on your Haders." They agreed and sped off back to Shonrar. "So what are we going to do then?" Dan was about to reply when Christian's Hader activated. It was Lord Stephen.

Lord Stephen: "Christian we need your help. We are under attack from more Boozemises."

Christian: “We are on our way.”

Lord Stephen: “Hurry, there are hundreds of them.” The communication ended but Christian could hear the chaos in the background before it cut out. He started pulling the reins to turn his griffin around, back to Shonrar. Dan had his eyes closed and was moving his head from side to side. When the griffin started moving he opened them and asked, “Where are you going?”

Christian: “Back to Shonrar, you heard the message there are hundreds of them, they will require our help.”

Dan: “No”, he closed his eyes again. “How many can you save if there is just you? We need to find the source of the problem.”

Christian: “That could take forever. My source thought there might be some in a cave in the Sandy Mountains.”

Dan: “No, this way.”

Christian: “Towards Leychr. We certainly won’t be welcome and we can’t fight them by ourselves if the bodies are somewhere in the castle.”

Dan: “We’ll worry about that when we get there. For now let’s just carry on.” They rode off.

Dignitaries

In Shonrar there was a mad panic as everyone was trying to flee from the Boozemises. Although they looked like rotting corpses, they had the ability to change into their old forms for short amounts of time. This was long enough for their families at home to let them in, thinking the returning member was alive and not dead from battle. Only then did they reveal themselves. Most of the Boozemises were just biting their victims and then moving on, but at the festival where the competing teams were, they were more bothered about killing the contestants. At the first sign of trouble the dignitaries were ordered to retire to their tent and stay there until they were told it was safe to leave. As a few of them peeped out they could see all the Boozemises running about. One walked past the tent, looking in. The two peepers fell to the ground and scrambled away from the doorway. The shadow of the corpse lingered only for a second and then moved on.

Dignitary 1: "It saw us didn't it?"

Dignitary 2: "Yes, I'm certain it did."

Dignitary 1: "So why didn't it come in?"

Dignitary 2: "I don't know." A voice from behind them joined in.

Dignitary 3: "Maybe the being controlling them knows who we are and knows we are worth more to them alive." He said calmly.

Dignitary 1: "You know I think he's right."

Dignitary 2: "I agree."

Suddenly someone ran into the tent and the two dignitaries screamed. The two of them were huddled together on the floor when a voice asked it they were all right. They looked up to see Joshua and Dean, two of the Shonrar leaders who were their friends. They held their hands out to help the dignitaries up.

Dignitary 3: "What's going on?"

Joshua: "We are under attack from Boozemises."

Dean: "Is anyone in here hurt?"

Dignitary 3: "No, they don't seem to bother us in here. I think they're probably leaving us alone so they can use us to sell back to the highest bidder."

Joshua: "Well, if you're safe in here then stay together, away from the sides and we will be back when we have control of the situation."

Dignitary 3: "And how do you propose to do that; take control? There must be hundreds of Boozemises out there. Has anyone contacted the MPC for emergency assistance?"

Dignitary 1: "Yes, if you mention we are here they will send someone immediately."

Dignitary 2: "If not sooner."

Dean: "We can't. Our Haders are being blocked. There is so much interference we can't even contact those from Lilechem who haven't come to the festival to help."

Joshua: "The lack of communications we have in this part of Phosia is one of the points we are to raise with you next month in our general meeting."

Dean: "We must go, but we'll be back." The two of them left the tent fighting.

Underground

When Dan and Christian reached the Shonrar Lake, Dan got him to stop the griffin. Dan got off and was looking around, so Christian released the griffin by the lakeside to let it drink. Dan was staring down at the ground. He got on his knees and put his hands on the long grass, pressing it into the mud. "Are there any caves nearby, any entrances underground?"

Christian: "I'm not sure, why?"

Dan: "Because I think they're directly under us, but the earth doesn't look disturbed round here so I'm assuming there will be a tunnel or something leading to whatever is under us."

Christian: "How do you know this? I haven't taught you any tracking skills yet." He turned around and smiled "Well the earth thing was easy because there would be lots of holes if you were thinking about hundreds of bodies but as for knowing… well, hopefully knowing where the bodies are kept." Dan got to his feet and started looking around. It was like he hadn't been bitten but Christian knew this burst of energy wouldn't last long. Dan looked around. "I just have a feeling, but not a normal feeling; it's really powerful as though I'm being lead somewhere for something." He looked across the lake. "We need to be over there." He pointed to where he was thinking and the two of them took the griffin over to the other side. Once they got there, Dan got straight off the back of the griffin and headed for some rocks. They were overgrown with bushes. Dan put his hand into the hole between them. "Put your hand in here" he said.

Christian: "Why?" he put his hand in. "There's cold air coming out."

Dan: "It must be something to do with the lake. Let's go check it out." Dan pushed the branches of the bushes out of their way and then stepped into the tunnel he uncovered. "It's so dark in here, if only we had some fire."

Christian: "Ah, this is where I can help." He got Dan to hold a branch and then picked up some dry stones by the lake. He cracked them together until he made sparks that in turn ignited the branch.

Dan: "Nice one."

Christian: "See, I do come in handy for something." Dan passed Christian the branch and then picked up one himself and lit it from Christian's. They entered the tunnel and followed it downwards to a large cave where a waterfall ran under the lake.

Dan: "How does that work?"

Christian: "You mean the water flowing over the top and flowing under here?"

Dan: "Yes, you would have thought that the lake would all drain down here, like water going down a plug hole."

Christian: "Obviously not. The water must have to pass over the top of a bump or something that leads down here. The rest must flow straight past it to go where it needs to. So where to next?"

Dan: "I'm not sure. Where were we above ground when I was on the floor? It was the other side of the lake right? So we need to swim over and search over there."

Christian: "What about the torches? Shall I go back and get the griffin?"

Dan: "No, we don't have time and I don't know if it will fit through the tunnel. We'll have to try to keep them above water. Besides it is calm, we should be all right. Hold mine a minute while I get in." Dan looked to see how deep it was. It looks quite deep. He jumped in and his feet couldn't touch the bottom so he swam back to the surface and reached his arm up. "Yes it's deep. Pass me the torches while you get in. Don't jump though we don't want to splash them."

It was early afternoon and the sun shone through the hole above them at times, when the water wasn't passing through it. A rainbow, created by the sun's rays, shone the rest of the time into the water below them. They struggled over to the other side. Dan threw his torch onto the bank, but it went out on the cold, hard ground. He then took Christian's off of him and laid it over the top so it wasn't touching the ground. The two of them got out further up, so as not to wet the one remaining flame. They walked back over to them after shaking themselves off and Dan relit his from Christian's. "Erg, what's that smell?" Dan asked.

Christian: "I believe that is the smell of rotting flesh."

Dan: "Good, we're close then." The two followed their noses and headed into the caves. They didn't know, but watchful eyes were surveying their every move.

As they were walking through the cave, Dan asked Christian if he missed Maddox.

Christian: "Of course I do; he was my best friend. We were inseparable me, him and…" he looked at Dan, "erm …we were like you and Mal teamed up together. He is… I mean was a very scatterbrained Jenoan, but he was well respected by all of us and he was the best warrior in Shonrar, easily."

Dan: "I miss him too. I didn't know him that long but he was a nice man." They had stopped to think about their memories of him, when Dan noticed the entrance not far away. "I think this might be it up ahead."

Christian: "We should hurry. If the controller of these Boozemises has been able to bring back hundreds of Boozemises then they will probably be strong enough to bring Maddox back as well."

Dan: "But you decapitated him" he said putting his hand on the bandaged up wound.

Christian: "Yes, but until we destroy his remains he can be brought back again and again." They started to run while the beings watching them moved away.

Trapped

In Shonrar the competitors had fled to the feasting hall and locked themselves in. They were totally surrounded and had their escapes blocked off. Lord Stephen was amongst them and was trying to contact Christian. He couldn't get a good enough signal to reach him but somebody contacted him. "Hello"

Martin: "This is Martin, where are you?"

Lord Stephen: "We are trapped in the hall and surrounded. Where are you?"

Martin: "I'm outside with John, but we can't get to you."

Lord Stephen: "Back off before they come after you."

Martin: "No, it's OK we're safe. For now the Boozemises are just biting us and then retreating. Once they've bitten you they leave you alone."

Lord Stephen: "Whoever is behind this obviously is more bothered about creating a new army of dead beings than killing us off or trading us as slaves. The thing is I think they are trying to kill us in here. Three of the contestants have already been slaughtered. You need to find a way of getting us out before they break in just in case. Oh and how are the dignitaries?"

Martin: "They are safe for now. They are in their tent and the Boozemises aren't even going near them, Dean and Joshua tell us."

Lord Stephen: "Make sure they stay with them. We can't be having them hurt or killed by Boozemises… or even worse turned into Boozemises, knowing what they know, otherwise Phosia as we know it could be turned into a waste ground."

Martin: "We understand."

Lord Stephen: "Can you get in contact with Christian?"

Martin: "No, our signals are very short distance between Haders."

Lord Stephen: "If you can, try and get someone up into the tower. Maybe some height will allow us to be able to communicate better."

Wound

As Dan and Christian enter the cave where the bodies are, they are overcome with the stench of the decomposing bodies all slung on top of one another.

Dan: "This has been going on for a while. Look how many there are."

Christian: "That will be why there are so many up there." Christian leans over to set the bodies alight.

Dan: "What are you doing?"

Christian: "Destroying the bodies so that whoever is controlling them can't."

Dan: "Shouldn't we say something?"

Christian: "Our friends and family are dying up there. What do you want me to say?"

Dan: "That's true." He quickly bowed his head and began to pray. "Dear Lord please take the souls of the dead here and bring them to you. Amen." Christian was just looking at him, "Go on then torch them." Christian hurled his torch into the mass of bodies while Dan began lighting the bodies on the ground nearest them. "OK then let's go."

They turned around to see the roots of a tree growing down from the ceiling, "quick cut some off with your sword."

Christian: "What are you going to do?"

Dan: "Hold the light." The flames burned behind them "Oh yeah, never mind I'll help you." They slashed away with their swords and then lit the chopped off roots and flung them as far as they could into the heaps of bodies.

Christian: "Hold on, I thought you'd been bitten on your shoulder. Doesn't it hurt anymore?"

Dan: "No, actually it doesn't." Christian felt his head and said, "You don't have a fever either." Dan looked under his shirt at his shoulder. He poked and prodded it a bit. "It doesn't even hurt anymore." He told Christian. He carefully pulled off the bandage. "It's fully healed." He said smiling.

Christian: "We have to get you to Lilechem as soon as possible."

Dan: "Why? I feel fine now."

Christian: "Yes, you feel fine because you're turning into one of them. We have to hurry before the process is irreversible." Christian grabbed him by the arm.

Dan: "I'm fine", he said angrily and picked Christian up in his arms and threw him out of the cave into the underground lake. Dan suddenly came to his senses and ran to the lakeside. Christian was getting out at the far side. "I'm sorry, something just came over me and I didn't feel in control." Dan said apologetically.

Christian: "Hurry, let's go before you start biting me or something." They got outside the cave. Dan was followed by Christian, who tried to hit him over the back of the head with the base of his sword.

Dan: "What are you doing?" He asked, after dodging the blow.

Christian: "I'm trying to knock you out before you start biting me or doing something worse."

Dan: "Well, I'm not going to let you do…" Dan went dizzy for a moment so Christian took his chance and bashed him on the forehead, knocking him out. "Don't worry you'll have healed by the time we get there" he said to himself as he placed him on the griffin. "It's me who's got to be worried, of you waking up." He climbed onto the griffin and flew off to Lilechem.

When they arrived in Lilechem, Dan was waking up, so Christian once again whacked him, knocking him unconscious. This time it wasn't as hard a blow. When Dan awoke again he saw Christian behind bars sitting on a chair. He took a moment to come to his senses and he then looked around him. He then realised he was the one in the cell. He stood up and looked at Christian who was standing by the bars. A familiar voice was coming from behind a wall where Dan couldn't see. As he got nearer the face of Maverick appeared shouting at Christian to get back. He pulled him away just in time, before Dan scratched his eyes out with his fingernails.

Maverick: "You're going through some changes Dan. I'm afraid it's going to get worse before it gets better."

Christian: "He can understand what I'm saying then?"

Maverick: "Yes, but it's like he has two conflicting brains running at the same time. He is listening to you but then the darker side of him comes out at random times and is triggered by his emotions. Until the serum takes effect he will continue changing into a Boozemises."

Christian: "Then what, how long does this process take?"

Maverick: "It's hard to say. Different cases take different amounts of time. I'm not a doctor I just know from when one of my friends became a Boozemises. We managed to restrain him and then took samples to try and find a cure. I hated watching him being tested on but we now have something which means we can help all those infected in Shonrar."

Christian: "What's happening about that?"

Maverick: "Some soldiers have been sent with enough serum for two thirds of the city and the ingredients required if they need to make anymore. Dean got through to me earlier and then Lord Stephen has just contacted us to say the rest of the Boozemises are dying off. I told him you were here and fine." They looked at Dan struggling to keep his body from changing. "You're better to just give into it, Dan. The sooner you progress to the final stage the sooner the serum will begin to work."

Christian: "So he has to be in the final stage before he gets better?"

Maverick: "Yes, as long as the serum is administered before the final stage of the process, it is totally reversible. We've had several patients who have been admitted over the past few months. As far as we've seen, there have been no side affects, thanks to my friend's antidote."

Christian: "How long ago did he die?"

Maverick: "A few months ago, when all this started. We'd heard rumours about Boozemises in Phosia but we didn't believe it. We were just out on a routine patrol when…" Maverick falls silent and drops his head, "My partner and I were sent on a mission and the result was Spencer Island. I'm sure I don't need to explain it any further to you."

Christian: "No, with losing our leader, as well as so many others from Shonrar, because of what happened there I know better than most."

Maverick: "At least the bites which Dan and the others have are from Boozemises that have been brought back to life. We haven't found a cure for the other kind of Boozemises yet, but we're working on it. At least the problem is contained for now, so if we can learn more about this less violent strain of the disease, we maybe able to devise an antidote for the other infection from which your leader died."

Christian: "So is that it or will he have to have more treatment?" He enquired, changing the subject back to Dan.

Maverick: "Yes, he'll have a few months of follow up shots but after that he should be immune to it if he gets bitten again. The only problem is that it has no effect if you administer the drug before a victim is bitten, as we found out the hard way. Oh well, work in progress; speaking of which I have some things to do. I'll be back to check on the two of you in a bit. If you need anything there should be someone at the desk outside."

Christian: "Thank you."

Maverick: "You're welcome and I'm sure I don't have to remind you not to go near the cage. If he seems back to normal again let the attendant know and she'll check him for you." Maverick leaves the room.

Christian: "Hear that Dan? It shouldn't be long before you're out of here and we can go home."

Dan: "Don't talk to me like a child. I know what you're saying." Christian started speaking in his normal voice rather than the condescending one he had put on to try comfort Dan.

Christian: "Everyone at home seems to be doing OK. I spoke to Michael just before you woke up. He said there were about three fatalities and a large number of bites, but they are all treatable like you." Dan was rolling around on the floor and groaning in agony. Christian stayed and talked to him for a while. After an hour, Dan was lying silent on the floor when Christian re-entered the room. "Nurse" he called out. "Can you check on him for me?" The female nurse got out of her seat and went round the back of the room where Dan was situated. "I'll be there in a minute," she said to Christian. "You can wait round the front if you like." Christian stood outside of the cage. The nurse was already in the room. She had nothing on her but a stethoscope, no protective clothing or anything. Christian was about to question her as she went to kneel down by Dan when he sudden sprung to his feet from the child's pose he had been in and leapt at her. He went right through her body and knocked himself out on the wall. She pulled a needle out of her pocket and injected him in the butt with it and then disappeared. Christian not believing what he had seen got himself together and walked out of the room. The nurse came back to her seat and continued with what she was doing. "He's not cured yet," she said. "I've given him something to keep him quiet. He might have a bruise when he comes round now."

Christian: "How did you do that?"

Nurse: "What, oh the hologram thing yeah it's new, we got a grant from the MPC so we can restrain and administer medication to our more… challenging patients without getting hurt or even needing to be in the room. We just step in a booth thing round there and it's like you're in the room or wherever. Clever little thing."

Christian: "That's amazing. How does it work?"

Nurse: "Do I look like a technician to you? All I do is use the thing; I have no idea how it works. I just know I feel a hell of a lot safer than I used to. I still get a little jumpy when they come to attack until I remember I'm safe in the booth next door. We've got a fantastic medical centre here; the best on Phosia!"

Christian: "Right, well, I suppose we should be off then."

Nurse: "Listen, I know I shouldn't probably be telling you this but I overheard your conversation with Maverick earlier and he not telling you everything about the drug trials."

Christian: "Really, why what didn't he say?" he asked looking worried.

Nurse: "Don't worry. What he said before about your friend being cured was true, but he failed to mention…" she began to whisper; Christian leaned in closer, "...that not all the drug trials were successful. As a result, the uncontrollable aspects of the Boozemises meant they were a potential threat to the surrounding population, so they had to be sent to you know where" she said nodding at him.

Christian: "What Spencer Island?" She continued nodding. "So what will happen to them now?"

Nurse: "Well, they'll either survive or they won't. Boozemises can't swim so there's no chance they'll escape to shore and there is that MPC facility on the island to monitor for any possible escapees. So this means there are now three types of Boozemises out there; the ones that can be brought back from the dead, the incurable kind, and now the genetically altered Boozemises."

Christian: "Wasn't that just a rumour about the medical facility on Spencer Island?" He knew it was true really, but the general populous wasn't supposed to know about it.

Nurse: "I don't know, I hear a lot of things working here that I probably shouldn't do."

Christian: "I bet you do." Someone enters the room.

Nurse: "Yes sir, the patient is now in a suitable state to be transported home" she said trying to be inconspicuous but failing miserably, especially with the little wink she gave Christian after finishing her sentence.

SECTION 02
The Solitary Task

Life & Learning

Time passes in Phosia and the Falcon boys grow into teenagers. By the age of fourteen, Dan is like a Phosian born to their planet. He and the other boys form strong bonds in training and in their social time they spend all day together. As well as their physical training they are also taught about the history of Phosia and about their surroundings. They learn about the numerous different cultures and beings spread across numerous galaxies and about the Multidimensional Protection Council (the MPC) who govern all these known worlds.

Alemap treats Dan as a job. She is afraid to get too attached to him and doesn't want to replace his real parents because she hopes he will return to them one day.

Up in his mountain retreat, Maddox has also been teaching his boy new tricks, preparing him to attack Dan - his murderer. Bitter and alone, apart from his son's spirit and the occasional visit from his spies, Maddox plots his revenge and waits for the opportune time to strike.

Christian and the other fathers use their combined skills to prepare their sons and Dan and Mal as warriors of Shonrar. Christian is especially pleased with the way Dan appears to sense dangerous situations before anyone else and how in tune he is becoming with his surroundings.

Dan is often dreaming of home and his past life with his family. He has grown to accept the fact he may not get home and even if he does they may be gone by the time he returns.

Lord Stephen has been keeping a close eye on Dan and the rest of his peers and often gets progress reports from the fathers. As he rules Shonrar, he is increasing worried about the number of troops Rechly appears to be gathering. Until one day he decides he cannot wait any longer and sends for Alemap.

Action Plan For Dan

Alemap: "Yes my Lord."

Lord Stephen: "It is time."

Alemap: "Now, are you sure he is ready?"

Lord Stephen: "We will never be totally sure, but the dangers around us grow more perilous each day. I worry if we do not do something now it maybe too late."

Alemap: "What do you need me to do?" Christian enters the room.

Christian: "Sorry to disturb you my Lord. You sent for me?"

Lord Stephen: "Yes Christian, come in. This concerns you too. It is time for Dan's second task but I fear he will not be able to complete it if he is interrupted. Lilechem have agreed to send their army to Leychr to battle Rechly's soldiers. However I believe there will be more to fear than just these beasts."

Christian: "What would you have me do sire?"

Lord Stephen: "I have had a vision of what Dan is to do. In the mountains there are lots of dangers, including Milo. We believe him to be hiding in a cave somewhere in that region."

Alemap: "What if he runs into Milo?"

Lord Stephen: "Alemap, Dan's task is a solitary one; however I have agreed with the MPC Superiors that you shall be allowed to follow him. You must not let him know you are there, although he shall probably sense you anyway. Just make sure Milo or any of his followers do not interrupt the task. The shadow beasts protect him, so be careful what you say and where. They can posses any shadow the sun throws down on the ground. We have no way of telling the difference until they attack. We cannot destroy them but we can use light to keep them at bay."

Christian: "What would you have me do sire, go and fight alongside our Jenoan brothers and sisters in Leychr?"

Lord Stephen: "No, they will have to do this alone. As I said there are other dangers that may befall our young friend before he can complete his mission. Alemap shall take half of the Shonrar leaders, while you and the rest of the boys must protect them from outside help. You shall all go with Dan to the base of the mountains. From there, Dan and Alemap's team may climb to the top. From here Dan must go on alone. You must follow him at a safe distance. Christian, you and your group shall stay at the base of the mountain until they return."

Alemap: "What must Dan find?"

Lord Stephen: "I cannot give you that information. I am only permitted to tell Dan. Go now, both of you, and prepare yourselves. The soldiers of Lilechem attack at first light tomorrow." They begin to leave. "Christian, you must make sure none of the boys go to help Dan, they are cunning as you taught them to be. Alemap send him to me now. We have a lot to discuss." The two nod and then leave the room.

Mountain Base

At first light the following day, everyone sets off to the foot of the mountain. Dan, aware of what he must do, starts climbing.

Christian: "Hold up boy. A few things before you leave. Your sword will be of use to you but only when you are not climbing. Here is a sheath you can wear on your back for storing your sword."

Dan: "Thank you."

Christian: "These you wear round your legs. We call them mountain claws. They can be used as weapons, but are excellent for climbing. Stick them into the wall and they latch hold. Press the release at the base to pull them out. Good luck."

Alemap: "Right, be careful, we do not know who lives in these mountains so keep your wits about you and remember you are not allowed anyone to help you with this task."

Dan: "I understand. Thank you both." Mal comes over to say goodbye.

Alemap: "Don't be long, we want to reach the summit before it gets dark." Mal gives Dan his father's necklace from around his neck. "Here I want you to have this."

Dan: "No, I couldn't."

Mal: "Don't argue, you can give it me back when you return."

Dan: "Thank you. I'll be back before you know it." They hug and then Dan turns to Alemap. "Ready when you are."

Snowy Mountains

Dan begins his journey up the mountain with Alemap and some of the fathers. The others below watch him for a few moments and then begin making camp.

Christian: "Mal, why aren't you helping?"

Mal: "I don't understand why I can't go with him."

Christian: "It's just something he must do himself. Go help the others."

After a few hours of climbing Dan and the others reach the summit of the mountain. From here they can see deep into the Snowy Mountains. As the group begin to set up camp, Dan says goodbye to Alemap once again. "I can do this, can't I?"

Alemap: "Yes, I believe you can do anything you put your mind to."

Dan: "I don't know. I have these tasks to do and I don't know where to begin. It was only by chance I completed the first challenge."

Alemap: "None the less you did it against the odds. This will be no different. I know how hard you've been training and I know you can do it." They both pause for a moment. Alemap hugs Dan and says, "So go and do it." Dan starts walking off into the mountainous area wearing a fur coat, the sheath, with his sword on his back, and a sack containing about five days worth of food and water. The others wait half an hour and then follow his tracks. They hurry so that they can try catch up with him before it snows and the tracks are covered.

The Girl & The Dragons

After a few days in the cold and snow, finding shelter in caves at night, Dan passes above Rechly's kingdom. He looks down at the tiny castle and surrounding grounds. He is just about to carry on when he notices a light flickering. He uses his Hader to magnify the area and sees the light is coming from a cave in the Sandy Mountains. After a few moments he forgets about the light and continues on his journey. Alemap is not far behind him with her helpers. Dan knows they are there, but tries not to look in their direction. As he is walking away from the edge of the Snowy Mountains above Leychr, he hears someone screaming. At first he doesn't know where it is coming from. Alemap sends one of the Shonrar leaders to check what the noise is and make sure it isn't a trap. "Don't let him see you." She says in a mixture of whispering and shouting as the Shonrar leader hurries off.

Dan: "Hello, is there anyone there?"

"Help me!" a girl's voice cries back. It is a young sounding female's voice.

Dan: "Where are you?"

Girl: "Over here."

Dan: "Keep talking so I can find you." Dan follows the sound of the voice until he reaches a chasm. On the other side there is a cave. The voice calls out again. "Are you still there?"

Dan: "Yes, where are you? I can't see you."

Girl: "I'm down here." Dan lies down and peers over the rocks. He sees something below him struggling to free its leg. "I'm coming down, just hold on."

Meanwhile the leader returns to Alemap. "I can't see who or what it is without revealing myself. We'll have to wait until he climbs down the chasm and hope he can handle whatever it is."

Alemap: "Right let's go." They move to the edge of the Chasm. By now Dan has climbed halfway down with the aid of his mountain claws. There is an alcove just above where the creature is. Dan kneels on it to assess the situation. "What's wrong?"

Girl: "I have my leg trapped under some rocks and they are too heavy to move. Won't you help me?"

Dan: "Most likely, but I am wary this maybe a trap and you may be luring me down there so you can eat me."

Girl: "I don't eat Jenoans, I eat fish from the glacier! Please help me!"

Dan: "What is your name?"

Girl: "Tyra… please there are ice dragons in the area. I don't want to die."

Dan scans the area, but doesn't see any dangers. He carefully goes towards Tyra. As he gets closer he realises what he thought she was wearing is actually hair on her body. She is covered from head to toe, apart from her face. As he looks her in the eye, he sees no malice and decides to help her. He starts removing the rocks from her trapped leg. She is lying on her front with her left leg trapped. She cannot get up or roll over to move the rocks.

Dan: "How did you get like this?"

Tyra: "I was walking alone back to where I live, when there was a rock slide. I live in the cave up the next cliff face. I was shouting for my father's help but he doesn't appear to be back from fishing yet."

Dan: "Can you walk?"

Tyra: "I don't know, hold on. Ouch! I don't think anything is broken."

Dan: "I'll help you back to your cave."

Tyra: "Thank you. What are you doing in this region? Not many Jenoans come here unless they are in hiding."

Dan: "I'm not in hiding, I'm on a mission."

Tyra: "A mission?"

Dan: "Yes, to find a golden feather."

Tyra: "Mmm, I thought that would be why you were here, most Jenoan's lie about their reasons for coming here."

Dan: "Well I'm not Jenoan, I'm human."

Tyra: "Human, I've never heard of that species before. You must be from another planet?"

Dan: "I think so." They headed to the bottom of the cliff face and were about to climb up it when Dan stopped.

Tyra: "What's wrong?"

Dan: "Hold on a minute." Dan closed his eyes and turned towards some rocks. "I don't know what it is, but it's big."

Tyra: "What's big?"

Dan: "Quick, start climbing."

Tyra: "What is it?"

Dan: "Just climb." As he said this, a dragon appeared from behind the rock. "I must have been wrong. I thought we were in grave danger." He said as a little ice dragon walked round the corner. It sneezed and ice shot from its nostrils.

Hiding up above the chasm, Alemap's eyes opened wide as she saw the dragon moving towards them.

Tyra: "We are in danger; you were right, hurry on up here." Dan walked over to where the little dragon was. "What's so scary about you then, little dragon?" The little dragon looked quite bemused by the strange being walking closer to it. Without fear, it hopped nearer to Dan.

Tyra: "Look stranger, we must leave now…"

Dan: "Dan, that's my name."

Tyra: "Dan, listen wherever there is a baby dragon…" she began talking slower as she became eclipsed in a shadow, "…one of its parents isn't far behind." Dan suddenly stumbled backwards as the creature's head appeared, followed by its gigantic body. He started crawling backwards, as before in the Leychr castle garden, but the larger dragon was more interested in Tyra who was shouting at Dan to get away. She continued up the cliff side but knowing she wouldn't get away in time, Dan got to his feet and threw a rock at the dragon, which was about to attack his new acquaintance. The dragon turned towards him, a little shocked.

Dan: "Don't move or say anything, I'm going to try to get its attention." The dragon turned back towards Tyra so Dan threw a few rocks at it. At this, the dragon ran for Dan who was also running away from it. The dragon was inches away from Dan when it hit the floor and wined. Dan turned around, his hands over his ears from the noise. He noticed Tyra still grabbing on. "Now's your chance", he yelled, "Get up the cliff." Tyra scrambled to the top of the cliff and looked on as Dan tried desperately to get further up the face. As she was looking she saw Jenoans up on the rim of the chasm. She couldn't get a good look at them, but noticed that a rock had fallen from where they were onto the dragon's tail. The ice dragon was frantically trying to get its tail out but couldn't. The dragon now spotted the Jenoans way up above and knew they had trapped him. He spat icicles up over the chasm, some of which broke on rocks as they fell and shattered on the group, slashing their skin. They managed to avoid being skewered by the big icicles but had to retreat.

All the commotion alerted two shadow beings to their presence. While one stayed to watch what they were doing, the other went off at great speed to tell Milo there was something happening.

Dan had now managed to get to the same level as Tyra and was using the dragon's distraction to try and get to her. The dragon noticed something out of the corner of his eye and turned the ice attack on Dan. He kept on climbing, managing to dodge the ice and debris caused by smashing rocks. Tyra was standing by a cave entrance. She came into the creatures view and was spat at in rapid motion. She was knocked to the ground before any of them hit her. Dan had leapt for her and the next thing she knew, she was on the ground, slightly dazed. He knew they had to get deeper into the cave to avoid injury. They scrambled in and round a corner and sat up against a wall, watching the dragon's pitiful attempts to reach them. After a while the dragon desisted.

Dan To The Rescue

Tyra: "Now what do we do? We can't stay here forever, there isn't any food."

Dan: "We have to free the dragon; well, I have to free it."

Tyra: "Are you mad? It nearly killed us!"

Dan: "Do you have anything I can use to break that rock? Hopefully if we free it…"

Tyra: "Are you mad?" she reiterated.

Dan: "Look, the longer it's out there, the more upset it's going to get. We need to do something, otherwise we aren't going to get out of here and your father won't be able to get back in. It's already beginning to get dark."

Tyra: "I have some explosives we could use."

Dan: "You just happen to have them lying around?"

Tyra: "Well yes, my father uses them sometimes to blow holes in the ice for fishing."

Dan: "How powerful are they?"

Tyra: "What do you mean?"

Dan: "Well, we want it powerful enough to break the stone but not so powerful that it blows off the dragon's tail or hurts us."

Tyra: "I don't know, you will just have to put it on the rock and see."

The two waited until it got dark. Alemap and the other leaders were now back at their vantage point, observing the situation. Dan peeked outside the cave and they all hid. He could not see the dragon from where he was standing. He assumed it was lying down because he could still hear it breathing. He proceeded to the edge carefully, knowing it could be a trap. As he peered over the edge of the cliff he noticed the dragon was lying down but facing away from him. He was hoping it was asleep but he couldn't be sure, so he crept to the rock face and carefully and slowly climbed down. Sure enough the dragon was sleeping, tired out from struggling and fighting. In its arms was its baby, huddled in a ball. When Dan got to the bottom of the cliff, he unintentionally made enough noise to wake the baby up but the father didn't stir. So Dan kept on with what he was doing. He turned away from the dragons to try and concentrate. He looked up the rock face to where Tyra had returned from her home with some explosives. She threw them down to Dan and he caught them. The little baby dragon, unlike its parent who was blue, also had red scaly skin. He sneaked up behind Dan who had laid out the explosive and was trying to light it. Dan turned round to see the little dragon jumping at his leg. He shook it off and it stood further back. It watched Dan, who was now facing the other way to watch for its father waking up. He tried lighting the fuse with some rocks, as Christian had shown him. It didn't light up straight away, but when it did Dan leaned over to the dynamite to see a slow burn down the long fuse so as to give him plenty of time to get back up to the cave. He turned to see the little dragon being all noisy. He tried to quieten it down, but he couldn't and the father was starting to stir. Suddenly, the baby blew fire out of its mouth towards Dan as though it was sneezing. He ducked and it burnt through most of the fuse instantly. Dan had only one way to run, which was towards the big dragon. He picked up the little one, ran as fast as he could and hid behind the leg of the big dragon. The explosive went off and the big dragon let out a yell. It stood up and looked at its tail and then turned towards Dan who was holding the baby in his arms. The baby dragon looked up at his father and then looked away as though he had done something wrong. He scrambled, jumped out of Dan's arms to the floor and went to his Dad. The father turned his head from them both and looked at his tail again. He looked back at Dan and seemed to smile. He came up close to Dan and licked him all over with his big wet tongue. "Erm… you're welcome! For a minute I thought you were going to eat me." Dan said to himself. The dragon turned away and took a deep breath. He then turned back to Dan who knew something wasn't right. The dragon breathed on him with his icy breath, until Dan was frozen solid to the wall. The dragon clawed away at the ice on the wall until Dan was just left standing in an icy prison. He turned away from Dan to his child, put him on his back and then picked Dan up, horizontally, in his mouth and started walking away.

Dan's onlookers didn't know whether he was alive or not, but they couldn't take the chance so Alemap and the others followed the dragon, putting a long distance between them.

Tyra's Father Returns

Tyra was still hiding in the cave when her father returned from fishing. He called for her and she returned home.

Father: "What have you been doing girl, playing with my explosives?" he asked as the apparatus was over the cave floor. She told him what had happened.

Tyra: "...and now Dan has been taken away."

Father: "I would have been down here sooner but there were some Jenoans up on the chasm top, in front of me. I had to wait until they'd left before I set off down so they didn't find our home."

Tyra: "They already know. They saw me run in here and get explosives for Dan."

Father: "Yes, but from the outside it only looks like a cave, not a home."

Tyra: "I suppose, isn't there anything we can do to help Dan? He saved my life."

Father: "Not now. The strangers have moved off and I don't know where the dragons live, so we can't follow them either."

Tyra: "I hope he will be alright."

Dragon's Lair

Team 2

The team waiting at the bottom of the mountain are sitting around, within a circle of fire. The circle surrounds the whole campsite to protect them from the shadow demons or anything else that might attack them. In front of a large fire in the centre of the camp, Christian and Julian are telling a story about dragons to the boys: "The dragon's lair is a place few beings who cannot control dragons have seen and escaped from. The rumours are that it has many caves in which hidden treasures are kept. Those able to pass through the dragon's realm brought some here from Sundaw, the dragon planet: one a fire breather and one an ice breather. Before this time the red dragons and the blue dragons had not lived together in harmony. In fact, whenever they were together they would attack each other like enemies at war. But the two he brought from Sundaw were the mildest he could find, though savage when being attacked, they did not fight each other and rumour has it they had babies, thousands of them who live in caves up in this mountain range. Deep in the heart of these caves is the treasure but another guardian also protects it. For those brave enough to risk their lives when the dragons are asleep, there is one more test awaiting them. If they pass, they may leave with some treasure; if not the guardian of the treasure wakes the dragons in the treasury by sounding a golden gong."

Ryan: "How do you know about the dragon's lair, has someone survived to tell you about it?"

Christian: "Yes, one man did visit it and return. That's why he was Lord of this land because of his bravery and because he completed a task set for him; Lord Stephen's father."

Jake: "Who set the task?"

Julian: "The Multidimensional Protection Council. They initiate tasks in worlds for positions for which they know only the individual or group who is competent to complete the task, can achieve."

Corey: "So have either of you seen a dragon?"

Christian: "Not in real life, only on a Hader."

Julian: "Anyway, I believe you should all get some sleep now. Joshua, Simon and Dean will be on guard for the first part of the night and I will be with Christian later. It will be your responsibility to take the first watch in the morning so you better keep your wits about you and stick together." They all head off for their tents.

Mal & The Mountain

During the night Mal decides to try his luck and heads up the mountain after Dan. He sneaks passed the guards on duty easily. He reaches the first ledge on the mountain and is pulled up onto it by Christian.

Christian: "I knew at least one of you would try it and I assumed it would be you."

Mal: "Why won't you let me go after him?"

Christian: "You're too late now. He will be far from here and even if you did manage to reach him, Alemap and the others would stop you from communicating with him."

Mal: "They've gone with him, haven't they? I thought

you said they would be waiting at the top of the mountain."

Christian: "They won't be interfering with his progress, they will just be making sure his task is not disturbed and is carried out properly." They sit quietly for a few moments and stare off into the forest. The camp was set up at the mountain point where the sacrifice of Milo's son took place. The water flowing from inside the mountain, which had been diverted, was now flowing freely again and hid the entrance to the tunnels they had escaped down. While sitting up on the ledge, unable to sleep, Christian was contemplating what had happened and whether they could have done things in another way. Mal was a nice distraction from his own thoughts.

Mal: "I don't want to lose him too."

Christian: "You won't. He's very resourceful as you know." A shadow beast goes past nearby but doesn't stop to see what they are doing. He avoids the circle of fire and heads to Milo's cave at full speed.

Christian: "Did you see that?"

Mal: "What?"

Christian: "Nothing, I thought I'd seen something moving. I'm off to bed now before my shift. I suggest you do the same. You won't find them now. You'll just get lost and probably die. Do I have your word that you're not going to try this again?"

Mal: "Yes, I promise." As they both climb down, Christian puts a tracking device on Mal just in case. Mal takes one last look up the mountainside, hoping Dan is doing all right, before they return to their tents and go to sleep.

Team 1

After following the blue dragon for miles to its home, Alemap, John, Martin and Michael pitched up a tent in the surrounding cliffs as the dragon entered into what appeared to be its home. It was still carrying Dan in its mouth and the baby on its back.

Alemap: "We can't go any further; my Hader says there are hundreds of warm and cold blooded creatures in there. We haven't had much sleep either. Put the tents up and get some rest. I'll take first watch. Hopefully Dan will thaw out and escape. We'll know if he dies because his Hader will deactivate. As long as it is still active we can trace him."

The Dragons

Inside the dragons lair a female dragon breathes fire around Dan to melt the ice. He lies on the floor until his body temperature is raised and he can move again. In the cave there is ice coming from the entrance, up to the base of a forest hidden below the mountains. When he comes to, Dan is worried he could be the dragons' next meal so decides to make a run for the trees. As he runs he suddenly stops and turns round when he hears the dragons talking to him.

Blue Dragon: "There's no need to run, you're not food." Dan turned around gob smacked.

Dan: "I… I?"

Red Dragon: "Are you hungry, we could get you some food if you like?"

Dan: "I… I?"

Blue Dragon: "Yes, we can talk, normally we choose not to though. We don't need to talk with words, we can read each others thoughts."

Red Dragon: "It's a bit cold in here, shall we return to the garden? Please come this way."

Dan followed them to the forest. As they walked to the edge of a cliff Dan saw the dragon's children playing down below them amongst the trees.

Dan: "How does this place exist? I would have thought the ice would have stopped anything from growing."

Red Dragon: "This place was chosen especially for the both of us because I need the heat…"

Blue Dragon: "…and I need the cold…"

Red Dragon: "and we can both live quite comfortably in between here in the garden."

Dan: "Where does the heat for you come from?"

Red Dragon: "Past the Snowy Mountains there is volcanic land. Although it is not visible on the surface, underneath there is an active volcano. That's where I go."

Dan: "Won't it burn you if it erupts?"

Blue Dragon: "It would me!"

Red Dragon: "Not me; my body is immune to the high temperatures of a volcano and the smoke doesn't bother me either."

Dan: "It's bad for your health though."

Red Dragon: "Not for me, I breathe it all out again. My body doesn't absorb it, just the heat, which I store and use to heat myself when I am in places like this, though I use the energy up much faster when I'm outside in cold weather."

Blue Dragon: "The same goes for me, but in reverse. I can survive going to her volcano for a short while if I need her, but would die if I stayed too long. I could cool myself down for a bit but after that…" he shook his head.

Dan: "You're a bit like camels then?"

Blue Dragon: "What are camels?"

Dan: "Where I come from there are these animals that store water in humps on their backs. They can store it for ages because there isn't much water around where they are, in the desert."

Red Dragon: "I've been to all the deserts on Phosia and never met a camel. Do they live underground or have they been imported from another planet?"

Dan: "No, it's me that has been imported. I come from a planet called Earth, have you heard of it?"

Blue Dragon: "Can't say I have."

Red Dragon: "No, me neither. So you're not Jenoan then?"

Dan: "No, I'm human."

Blue Dragon: "Well, I don't know how that will affect the outcome." He whispers to his partner who shushes him.

Red Dragon: "Why are you here in the Snowy Mountains, little human?"

Dan: "My name is Dan. I'm here on a quest to find some gold." The two dragons look at each other.

Dan: "I have three tasks to perform so I can go home to Earth, one of which I am currently doing, is to find some gold."

Red Dragon: "Well, we can't help you. I'm sorry." She said abruptly.

Blue Dragon: "Hold on a second, let me just have a word with my partner a moment." They turn towards each other and Dan realises they must be talking telepathically because he can't hear them but can see the facial expression they are making.

Blue Dragon: "Don't be so hasty. He did rescue me after all."

Red Dragon: "That doesn't mean we should let him have some treasure. If we do that and let him go, he could bring others."

Blue Dragon: "He doesn't look the type; beside he's only trying to get home. Remember what we were like when we first arrived. We were home sick. If it hadn't have been for each other we would have probably died. Plus he has another task to do before he can get to any treasure."

Red Dragon: "Fine, but don't blame me if we get into trouble when the master knows more gold is missing." They turn to Dan and talk to him.

Red Dragon: "OK, I've decided..."

Blue Dragon: "Hmm"

Red Dragon: "...we've decided to let you in on a little secret. There is a temple in the middle of the forest. In there is a guardian of some treasure. If you pass the test he sets you, he will let you have a prize."

Blue Dragon: "I warn you now though, if you fail you could die."

Red Dragon: "We can help you..."

Dan: "No I'm not supposed to be helped with things physically."

Red Dragon: "I was just going to say we could guide you to the temple. We're not allowed to help you from then. We'll wait for you outside for a bit though. Tell the guy inside, Cornelius, to let us know if you don't survive please."

Dan: "OK" he says turning his nose up at their faith in him. "Let's go then."

Red Dragon: "I suggest you have something to eat and have a sleep first. You look tired. You can do the test tomorrow."

Dan: "OK then, I'll do that. I've been on my feet for days." The dragons offer him some food but he turns them down in favour of something he likes from his backpack. Afterwards he tries to get comfortable, but soon falls asleep from exhaustion.

Milo

Up in his cave, Milo is training his son in weaponry and other skills using the Yashel. It is the middle of the night and a shadow being pays him a visit.

Shadow: "Master."

Milo: "What is it? I'm busy."

Shadow: "There is something I think you should know."

Milo: "Well, what is it?"

Shadow: "Alemap and some others are camped out at the mouth of the dragons cave. One of them has gone in."

Milo: "That's foolish of them. They know they won't survive in there long. Anything else?"

Shadow: "More of them are camped out at the bottom of the Snowy Mountains."

Milo: "Interesting, but still, what does it have to do with me?"

Shadow: "The boy who went into the cave…"

Milo: "A boy?" He stops training. "We shall have to finish this later my boy." He takes his hand out of the Yashel. "Continue, what about the boy?"

Shadow: "He was wearing Maddox's necklace."

Milo: "Damn! Still not the right one, but I am curious as to why they would send the dead mans son in; it could be a distraction to his real task. I will go; you say there are more at the bottom of the mountain pass. Fine. The dragon's lair is nearer to Leychr anyway. I shall pass through that way. Come with me, you shall be my guide. It's been along time since I went to the dragon's cave."

Shadow: "Very well master. You will not be there till morning, so I will meet you at the top of the mountain where I can hide in the shadows."

Milo: "I will be there before morning, but go, I shall meet you there." The shadow being leaves and Milo calls upon a giant bird to carry him to Leychr. It does not take long but he sees guards from Lilechem camped out in the woods near Leychr. As he lands, the bird flies off again. Milo walks freely through the castle and goes to talk with Rechly.

Rechly: "How dare you show your face here?" He yells.

Milo: "Shut it you fool and listen."

Rechly: "How dare you come to my kingdom and insult me. You will be killed for your insolence." Milo is attacked by several of Rechly's subjects, but uses magic to suspend them in mid air.

Milo: "You are the one who couldn't deliver on his end of the bargain. Don't blame me."

Rechly: "Because of you, my brother is dead. Teburnt, Teburnt."

Milo: "Because of you, my plans have been hindered and the murderer of my son walks free. How hard can it be for a pack of thousands to kill ten young boys? Oh, but let me guess, you weren't planning on killing them anyway, just selling them off to the highest bidder." Rechly looks guilty. Milo gets angry too. His magic starts to wear off so he pushes the beasts out of the way. "I give you simple instructions but even you can't follow them." The beasts that attacked Milo get to their feet but move to the sides of the room out of his way.

Rechly: "I no longer care about what you have to say. Teburnt is dead."

Milo: "Teburnt and Maddox have been dead for a long time. Stop wallowing in self-pity and do something about it."

Rechly: "What can I do? I can't bring back the dead. You of all Jenoans should know that after losing…" Milo comes running up to him and slaps him round the face.

Milo: "Don't you even say his name! If you had helped me when I asked, I could have saved him. Now I have to resort to…" he stops and realises he doesn't want to reveal his plans to Rechly so changes the subject. "I have business in the Snowy Mountains; allow me access to the path up the mountain."

Rechly: "Why should I do that?"

Milo: "Because you have more important things to worry about."

Rechly: "Like what?"

Milo: "Like the thousands of Lilechem soldiers camped

outside in the Shonrar woods. They are coming for you."

Rechly: "You are lying; even Lilechem doesn't have an army that big."

Milo: "Maybe I exaggerate a little. Or maybe they have help."

Rechly: "Shonrar. Guards? Bring everyone here now."

Milo: "There's nothing you can do. In a few hours it will be first light and then they shall be upon you like a swarm."

Rechly: "What do we do?"

Milo: "Do I have your permission to use the passageway?"

Rechly: "Yes, yes. Tell me."

Milo: "You must clear the castle. Use the underground passages and go to the Sandy Mountains. Take weapons and food with you, but nothing else. You will need to move swiftly to get all your, huh, creatures out of here before dawn. Listen to me now you pathetic fool." Milo gets up close to him again. "Do not take all your treasures with you; leave it all, because if my plan works you won't require them because you will have Lilechem's instead."

Rechly: "You can do that?"

Milo: "Possibly. If everything goes to plan, then I can have so much more." His eyes grow larger as he thinks of what he could gain and Rechly believes him.

Rechly: "Like what?"

Milo: "Hmm? Never you mind just concentrate on not

getting captured and don't leave anyone behind. We don't want them to find where you have gone, yet. Now take me to the pathway I must hurry."

Rechly: "Right away, after one more question, your boss? What happened when they realised they weren't getting the jar thing?" They head for the tunnel.

Milo: "Oh that, well I've stalled them for now, but if my plan works I'll have something even better to give to them."

Rechly: "And if it fails?"

Milo: "Plan B; I have obtained something called a Shafellor. I don't quite know what it does yet, but it was costly and my sources tell me it is well worth the price. I'm sure someone as well connected as my boss will have the resources to find out what it's used for."

The Temple

The next morning Dan woke up a bit achy, but not where he was when he went to sleep. "Where are we?" he asked, from the back of the blue dragon.

Blue Dragon:	"We are on our way to the temple. We thought we'd set off early because there is a river we must cross further up stream."
Dan:	"Can't we just swim across?"
Red Dragon:	"We could, but there are other creatures in it at this time of day. They come to bathe in the morning but are gone by midday. We thought we'd walk you round so you could see more of our garden."
Dan:	"That sounds good. I'm not really in a rush."
Blue Dragon:	"So why don't you tell us about Earth."
Dan:	"Well I come from a place on Earth called England. Normally it's quite cold and wet but it's nice. I live…"

By this time, Milo had reached the top of the mountain and come out behind the shadow creature. "Are we going then? For my plan to work I need to be at the dragon's lair as soon as possible."

Shadow:	"Where did you…? OK let's go, this way."
Milo:	"This way, actually."
Shadow:	"The dragon's lair is this way."

Milo: "I know and I have transport to get us there."

At the foot of the temple, the dragons left Dan and went to bathe in the water. A well-rested Dan went on into the temple.

Red Dragon: "Do you think we'll ever see him again?"

Blue Dragon: "Well he isn't from this planet, so who knows, maybe humans aren't greedy creatures like those of Phosia."

As Dan entered the temple, there was a dark passageway leading to the main part of the temple. He proceeded through the passageway, carrying a burning torch from the front entrance. It was a very old building covered on the outside by wild plants and surrounded by the trees. Inside, it was riddled with cobwebs and the stones on the floor were being pushed up by weeds growing under them. At the end of the corridor there were some doors. He opened these and entered into the main part of the temple, where Jenoans would have come to worship at one time. Since Dan knew nothing of the temple's history, he didn't know who had built it or worshipped in it. The ceiling in the middle of the room had caved in and gone through the floor below. There were birds inside the room and as he got nearer to the hole, he could see animals in the trees above him in the distance. He wasn't looking where he was going and tripped over a rock. He fell forward down through the hole in the floor. He rolled a few feet down. When he stopped rolling he couldn't see much but the light above him. The torch with the flame burning on it was at the top of the hole but slightly out of reach. Dan tried getting out but he couldn't make it to the top of the hole. He looked behind him to where the darkness consumed the far side of the hole in the floor where the sunlight couldn't reach and was thinking he could do with some light. To his surprise his Hader began emitting light and he flung the arm with his Hader around thinking something was on him. When he realised what it was he felt a twinge in his arm as he remembered some of the things Jenoans had told him about the uses of his Hader. He remembered that the Hader was in tune with his biological systems and that he could access many different features through it. He thought the light should be brighter and it was. Looking around he saw it was only a small room and believed it to be a dead end until he noticed a bit of cloth caught on a wall. As he went to investigate, he found it was a trick of the light that the room was a dead end and that round the corner was a tunnel. He knew he couldn't get out the way he came in without help so he followed the tunnel further down into the temple, looking for another exit. As he reached the bottom of the tunnel, it lead forward on a level gradient and at the end was at door with light emitting from the edges. He proceeded to the door and pulled on the handle.

The Keeper Of The Treasure

The door was old and squeaked as it moved. As he opened the door the room behind it shone with thousands of pieces of gold and other treasures. His Hader switched off and Dan couldn't believe his eyes. He heard a noise behind a mound of gold so he called out but there was no reply. He went a bit nearer to investigate, but sensed danger so he kept his hand on his sword. "Hello; is there someone there?" he asked again. This time an old man came out from behind the mound. "Why, hello there young sir, and how can I help you?"

Dan: "I have come seeking a certain piece of gold for my Lord."

Old Man: "Well, as you can see there is plenty of gold here."

Dan: "Before I forget, the dragons said to tell them if I don't return."

Old Man: "Dragons? Are they here now?"

Dan: "No sir, they cannot enter the Temple."

Old Man: "Of course, silly me. I'm getting a bit mad in my old age you know. So how much gold do you want?"

Dan: "Well Sir, I'm looking for a certain piece of treasure; a golden feather."

Old Man: "A golden feather, you say. Well I haven't seen one but you're free to look for it. I'll help you if you like."

Dan: "Thank you."

Old Man: "Let's start over here. That's a nice necklace you're wearing."

Dan: "Thank you."

Old Man: "Is it yours?"

Dan: "No, it belonged to someone very special to me."

Old Man: "Who?" Dan saw something that looked like a feather.

Dan: "What's that?" he went to look but it was something else. "Ha, I thought for a moment this was a feather." Then something else caught his eye. It was a large golden-framed mirror. "Wow, that's beautiful!"

Old Man: "Ah yes and this is a special mirror. It can transport you anywhere you would like to go; one way of course."

Dan: "Anywhere?"

Old Man: "Yes. Is there somewhere you want to go?"

Dan: "Well..." Dan turned around to him and he saw what he had been looking for behind the old man, in the distance. "There it is."

Old Man: "What? Your home?"

Dan: "No, the golden feather." It was lying beyond the mound of gold the old man had appeared from.

	He ran towards it."
Old Man:	"Wait, don't go up there." But he was too late; Dan had already reached it. He picked it up and turned round. The old man got to the mound and looked behind it. He looked a bit shocked.
Dan:	"Are you alright?"
Old Man:	"Yes, I just thought I'd, erm, left my glasses round here somewhere." Dan walked back towards the mirror. The old man looked around and saw a shadow being by a door, hidden by golden coins. He gestured with his hand as to shoo the being away. Dan saw him gesturing but could not see the door or shadow being for the mound. The old man walked back towards Dan and the mirror.
Old Man:	"So then, what else do you want?"
Dan:	"I don't, I have what I came for now."
Old Man:	"That's it?"
Dan:	"Yes. I only came on behalf of Lord Stephen. Now I must return this to him and I shall have fulfilled my mission."
Old Man:	"What's Lord Stephen up to?" he whispered under his breath.
Dan:	"Did you say something?"
Old Man:	"Yes, if this is for him then what would you like?"
Dan:	"Nothing."
Old Man:	"There must be something you desire?"
Dan:	"Well, I would like to go home." He put his hand on the mirror and an image of his home on Earth appeared. Dan didn't notice it as he

turned to ask the old man a question. "What is the test I have to pass?"

Old Man:	"Test, erm, there isn't one today, I'm feeling generous." Dan saw he was looking at the mirror in a confused way, so he turned around to see what it was showing. Dan gazed longingly into the mirror. He didn't dare put his hand through the mirror straight away so he threw a dagger lying on the floor by his feet. "Where did you say you were from?" The old man asked.
Dan:	"I didn't. A place called Earth." The old man quietly drew a knife from a sheath on his leg and started to walk up to Dan.
Old Man:	"Earth? Where is that? It's been so long since I've been out into Phosia because of those dragons..." Dan grew suspicious after believing he and the dragons were friends.
Dan:	"What did you say your name was?" he began to turn around, so the old man hid the knife behind his back.
Old Man:	"I didn't, I am the Guardian of the Treasure, I have no other name." He stops where he is and decides there is another way to get rid of Dan. "Don't you miss your home?"
Dan:	"Very much." Dan replied. Knowing he is not who he is supposed to be, Dan tried to figure out who he is.
Old Man:	"Why don't you go home now? Just think of your home again and walk through the mirror." Dan suddenly sensed the presence of more beings.
Dan:	"I have a duty to get this back to Lord Stephen."
Old Man:	"Or you could take the gold with you. You've

been away from home a long time haven't you? Why not leave now, while you can and take that bit of treasure as an added bonus?" Dan thought about it for a few seconds.

Dan: "I could, but Lord Stephen and the others are relying on me. I need to do this. I have a duty to them, whether I like it or not and hopefully when I have fulfilled that duty I can return home. I wouldn't feel right leaving them in trouble and not getting to say goodbye, they're like family to me now."

Old Man: "Fine, we'll have to do this the hard way." The old man's voice suddenly changed, as it was really Milo who had been pretending to be the treasurer.

Milo VS Alemap

He pulled his knife on Dan, who reached for his sword on his back. "Oh no you don't!" Milo said, now close enough to him to hold the knife at his throat. "At first, I thought you were Maddox's son, what was his name? Oh yes, Mal. This is what confused me." He grabbed the necklace, pulled it from his neck and flung it into the piles of gold behind him. "You should have just gone back where you came from. I should slit your throat right now, but I have plans for you."

Dan: "Plans? I'm not going to work for you. I don't know who you are but I know I don't trust you."

Milo: "You don't know who I am? You think you can get away with murder and just walk away?"

Dan: "Murder, what are you talking about?" Just then Alemap appeared from behind the mound of treasure, closely followed by an old man.

Alemap: "OK Milo, it's over." She walked towards them while the old man quivered behind a mound of silver. Dan knocked the knife out of Milo's hand as he pushed him to the ground. Milo went for the knife as Alemap approached him.

Milo: "Alemap, where did you come from?"

Alemap: "The same way as you, by the looks of it." She drew her sword.

Dan: "What are you doing Alemap? Be careful!"

Alemap: "Don't worry about me." She turned to Milo who also drew a sword. "Time to settle some differences don't you think?"

Milo "I've been looking forward to it."

Alemap lunged for Milo first; he blocked her advance towards his chest. They began clashing swords.

Milo: "Straight for the heart, that's understandable."

Alemap: "Well, no use messing around. We have been busy with the Boozemises at our mid-summer festival. I assume that was your doing?"

Milo: "Well, I had a little help." Dan was sitting on the floor amazed at how good Alemap's fencing was. She was definitely better than he was.

Alemap: "Is this why we haven't heard much of you lately? Controlling hundreds of Boozemises at once must have taken a lot out of you?"

Milo: "It did. It would have been easier if I had my sceptre, but you stole that so I had to make do. Enjoying my old job? You can't be half as good as I was."

Alemap: "You were too big for your boots. You had to be taught a lesson."

Milo: "And you were the one to do it." Alemap lunged towards him. He moved out of the way and she fell towards him. He got her round the neck with his arm and held his sword at her with the other hand. He whispered, "The boy is all right" in her ear and smelt her hair. She struggled to get away from him.

Dan got to his feet and picked up a silver vase lying on the floor. He hit Milo over the head with it while he was facing away from him. He was shocked enough to release his grip on Alemap. She punched backwards hitting him in the face, by leaning downward to her left while her right arm came up and smacked him on the jaw. She then moved out of his way. He turned and pushed Dan out of the way of the mirror, grabbed the nearest box of treasure he could find, placed his hand on the mirror and thought of his cave. Alemap threw a knife at him, barely missing him. It passed through the mirror and stuck into a cupboard door in his cave. Milo kicked another small chest through the mirror and then walked through himself with the larger chest under his arm. Dan got to his feet and was about to go after him when the doorway closed and Dan walked into the mirror.

Dan: "Aww, my nose." He cried.

Alemap: "Well Dan you've completed your task so we can go home now."

Dan: "Who's the old man?" he said rubbing his nose.

Alemap: "This is Cornelius. He's the real treasurer of this place."

Dan: "I'm not quite sure what just happened here."

Alemap: "I saw Milo ride up outside the dragon's lair and he took the back entrance into the treasury with a shadow being."

Dan: "How did he know about that?"

Alemap: "He's been here before, with Lord Stephen."

Dan: "Wow. I didn't know they knew each other."

Alemap: "I'll explain their connection later. As for now, by the time I got to the cave entrance, the shadow being was bringing Cornelius up the stairs. I had been hiding outside when he dumped his body on the sleigh pulled by mountain wolves that he and Milo had arrived on. I left the rest of the group to distract and deal with it while I helped Cornelius back down here."

Cornelius: "Yes, and we heard what happened. You did well, my boy."

Dan: "My boy. That's what he kept calling me."

Cornelius: "Well, he has met me in the past." Dan looked down at the golden feather. "You can keep that, you've earned it."

Dan: "So, if you're the real Cornelius then give me the task. I haven't done it yet and I'd feel bad about it if I just took this."

Cornelius: "But you have done it my boy. The test was to see if you could resist taking more than you deserve. You passed up the chance to go home."

Dan: "So what's going to happen to him?" He asked pointing towards the mirror.

Cornelius: "Normally, I would have taken care of him but he came in the back way, which I wasn't expecting. Very few know about it and I was distracted watching for you coming from the other direction. He's a changed Jenoan from when I met him the first time."

Dan: "He called me a murderer!"

Cornelius: "Well I don't know anything about that, though you don't look the type. Normally you can see it in their eyes."

The Mirror

Alemap: "We have to go now; the shadow being might bring reinforcements. We have to close the tunnel off at the top so they can't find it."

Cornelius: "You're too late. It has already been done. The back entrance to the tunnel has been moved. Use the mirror to get back home."

Alemap: "We can't, I've left men outside waiting for us so we should go there."

Dan: "Can I go back to my world from here?"

Alemap: "Dan, you can't go. We need you."

Dan: "Do you? I've been here seven years. I know I've achieved a lot here, but I miss my family, my Mum and Dad will be thinking I'm dead and I even miss my sister. Huh, it takes being sent to a different world to realise how much you don't appreciate the ones you love when they are around. I want to stay but I want to go home too. I'm tired of having to be alone in what I do. I know I have all your support but I'm not like the other boys. This isn't my world."

Alemap: "I understand. If you have to leave I'll miss you, but I can't keep you here if you really want to go."

Cornelius: "Well, you can't use this mirror to get yourself home just now anyway."

Dan: "Why?"

Cornelius: "Well, Alemap threw that dagger through the mirror portal."

Dan: "Yes and…?"

Cornelius: "Well, for the portal to open to a world as far away as yours, it requires a lot of power. Once the door closed, the mirror set itself on recharge. The knife was actually a key to use the mirror for long distance and dimensional travel. It's what we in the know call a Cepren."

Dan: "How long before the mirror will have charged up enough to get me home?"

Cornelius: "Not too long, just about ten years, give or take a few."

Dan: "Ten years, I can't wait that long."

Cornelius: "I'm afraid you'll have to, but you can go anywhere in Phosia. It doesn't use a lot of power here."

Alemap: "Let's go outside then, the men will be worried about us." She heads to the mirror.

Dan: "Can they wait a bit? I have a few friends I want to say bye to first. Come on, this way. Goodbye Cornelius. Thank you."

Cornelius: "You're welcome my boy. Stay safe the both of you and good luck on your quest."

After testing that he can go through first, Dan pulls Alemap through the mirror and they appear in the river outside the temple. The two dragons are outside still waiting. "I'm back." They see Alemap and look to each other. Dan knows they are talking to each other so he puts their minds at ease. "Don't worry, she's a friend, you can trust her." They look at each other again and then at Dan. They begin talking to him, but in his head.

Blue Dragon: "We would talk to her, but it is impossible for us to do so unless we know we can trust her."

Dan: "Wow, how are you doing that?"

Red Dragon: "We can talk to you because you proved you're worthy of our trust. If you like, we can take you back to the cave entrance and cut through the river way too."

Dan: "If you don't mind."

Red Dragon: "Tell your friend I'm going to lift her on my back."

Dan: "Alemap come over here. The red dragon is going to give you a lift on her back."

Alemap: "How do you know that and how do you know it's a she?"

Dan: "They've been speaking to me; in my head that is." The dragons lifted the two of them onto their backs and proceeded to the cave front.

Dan: "Thank you for all your help."

Blue Dragon: "You're welcome."

Red Dragon: "Come back and visit sometime."

The Journey Home

In the cave in the Sandy Mountains, Milo empties out the gold and other items from his treasure chests. Talking to his son in the Yashel, he is very pleased with himself. "Well my son, your father has been good to you. I have enough treasure here to get all the things I need to bring you back, with some left over for me too. Oh, and you were right. The boy, he has been infected, he just doesn't realise it yet."

As the team headed back to those at the base of the mountain, Christian was voicing his worries to Julian.

Christian: "We should have heard some noise from Leychr by now. The Lilechem army were supposed to attack at first light. We should have heard battle noises by now, we're directly down wind of it."

Julian: "Maybe they are having trouble gathering their army and are waiting till later in the day?"

Christian: "If that was true they would have sent a message to Shonrar and we'd have been contacted."

Julian: "So what do we do?"

Christian: "We wait for the safe return of the others and then check with Shonrar. If they haven't heard anything we shall go ourselves to Lilechem."

Alemap and the others are using the sledge that Milo left behind in his hasty retreat. Dan is sitting next to Alemap.

Dan: "So tell me how Lord Stephen and this Milo knew each other."

Alemap: "Well, I am Milo's predecessor. He used to be the know it all man and I was one of his apprentices."

Dan: "Who were the other apprentices?"

Alemap: "There were a few but they moved on to other places, like Lilechem, but he died in a Boozemises attack."

Dan: "So if Milo was your trainer then he was a good guy?"

Alemap: "You mean he was on our side, yes. He was a much loved 'person' in our little community."

Dan: "What happened to Milo to make him bad?"

Alemap: "He was angry that his son was killed. He became hostile and was banished from fear of what he could and would have done to Shonrar."

Dan: "How did it happen?"

Alemap: "What?"

Dan: "How did the boy die?" Michael looked at Alemap and then hung his head down.

Alemap: "He burnt to death."

Dan: "That's terrible. I think I'd rather freeze to death than be burnt. Although I suppose it would be faster." Alemap was getting a bit touchy on the subject and decided to carry on with the story with a little prompt from Michael.

Michael: "Tell him about Maddox."

Alemap: "Ah yes. Maddox and Milo were great friends. In fact, the necklace you are wearing it was chosen for him by Milo. He treasured it and it has been a reminder of their friendship ever since."

Dan: “Does Mal know that?”

Michael: “No, he doesn’t. Maddox didn’t want him to know after Milo turned nasty. He also gave Lord Stephen a necklace too.”

Alemap: “One day the two of them, Lord Stephen and Milo, discovered the cave with the dragons in. Back then there were far fewer than there are now. They managed to escape because the female was giving birth. When they got outside the cave they hid hoping to escape the blue dragon when it came out. That’s when they found the back entrance to the cave.”

Dan: “So it was an accident they found it?”

Michael: “Yes, but a most fortuitous one as it turns out. At the bottom of the passage they found the room with gold in. Again, it will probably have had a lot less than it has now.”

Alemap: “They met Cornelius in there, but obviously Milo hadn’t remembered his name when he saw him this time.”

Michael: “From what they told us, Cornelius said they could both have one item each from the treasury to leave with. Milo tried to convince Lord Stephen to take more or to come back with more Jenoans but Cornelius changed the entrance while they were in there and said he would again once they left. Lord Stephen wouldn’t allow Milo to take more than had been offered to them. This then became the test for those who were seeking the gold whether they would be overcome with greed or whether they could resist.”

Alemap: “Milo brought back a golden sceptre with a jewel held on the top, which he used as a catalyst with his magic, while Lord Stephen brought back a jewelled crown which he used as a symbol for being the Lord of the land."

Dan: "I'm confused, how could he have done all this? He would only have been young."

Alemap: "Sorry, of course you won't know. The Lord Stephen you know is Lord Stephen junior. The one we are talking about is..."

Dan: "...Lord Stephen's father."

Michael: "That's right. The title then went to Lord Stephen when his father died, along with the crown, although he hasn't worn it yet, probably because he is still in mourning over his father's death."

Dan: "What happened to the sceptre?"

Alemap: "We still have it. It is kept safe in our treasury."

Dan: "Do we have a lot of gold?"

Alemap: "I think that's a question you should ask Michael. I haven't seen the treasury. Only the Shonrar leaders are permitted entry."

Michael: "and Lord Stephen of course."

Simon: "We're nearly there now Alemap; we should dismount here and release the wolves."

Alemap: "Do it, we must get down the mountain quickly. Our services maybe required in Leychr."

Return To The Mountain Base

After being at the bottom of the mountain for the fifth day, movement was finally spotted below snowy peaks.

Dean: "Christian, Julian, I see something up there. I think it's them." Everyone came to the base of the mountain to try and see them. It was bright and they had to hold their hands over their faces. Sure enough, as they got nearer, Julian counted all the members that had gone up, as they descended to meet them. The ground team helped them down and Mal and the other eight boys ran straight over to Dan to see what he had been up to. Dan passed the necklace back to Mal.

Mal: "So how was it?"

Dan: "Tiresome."

Mal: "You've missed some useful training while you were away."

Jordan: "We've been learning to start fires…"

Graeme: "…and how to hunt animals…"

Corey: "…and we even got to take watch by ourselves!"

Jake: "I think they might have been keeping an eye on us though."

Ryan: "What about you?"

Matthew: "Yes, there must have been some interesting adventures up there."

Dan: "Well, I was attacked by a dragon."

James: "A dragon? Did you slay it?"

Dan: "No, but I did rescue it after it got trapped and he had such a cute baby."

Ben: "How do you know it was a he?"

Dan: "Because he spoke to me. Well, not all the time, sometimes he used his mind."

The boys walked off to the main fire area to continue catching up, whilst Dan told them how big the dragon was.

Christian: “So it went alright then?”

Alemap: “Yes, I’d say so.”

Michael: “Apart from Milo showing up.” Christian’s Hader activated.

Christian: “It’s Lord Stephen. Excuse me a minute.” He started walking off. After a few moments he walked back in their direction. “Yes, Dan is fine and Alemap is too, yes.”

Lord Stephen: “Good. I shall see you all back here soon then.”

Christian: “Yes, bye… so Milo, what’s it got to do with him?”

Alemap: “I think he may know about Dan.”

Christian: “Is it going to cause problems?”

Alemap: “I’m not sure.” Michael goes over to the boys. “Right you lot, you can tell each other stories later. Let’s get this lot packed up and get home.”

Alemap: “There’s one thing for sure. Dan’s last test will be the hardest he’s faced yet.”

Christian: “Do you think he’ll be able to pass it?”

Alemap: “I don’t know what it is, but he’s definitely shown strength in character as well as his survival skills.”

Christian: “Do you think we should tell him about ‘You Know Who’ yet?”

Alemap: “No, I don’t think he’s quite ready.”

Christian: “What about the boys?”

Alemap: “They know a little, but they don’t know enough.”

Christian: “They don’t know that Dan killed Milo’s son.” He walked over to the boys, “Come on then let’s go.”

SECTION 03
21

Several more years have passed in Phosia and it is coming up to Dan's twenty-first birthday based on the day he arrived in Phosia at seven. A lot has changed since the adventures in the Snowy Mountains. All the boys are now young men and have surpassed Christian's expectations in their training. Leychr has been deserted all this time. No one from Shonrar or Lilechem knows where the Leychrians have all vanished to, though there are a variety of different theories. There are a few guards posted between Shonrar and Lilechem and communication between the two cities has greatly increased thanks to a new law which dictates that all creatures under MPC control must wear Haders or be tagged with similar devices.

Milo has also been busy learning new tricks with the Yashel. He kidnapped a young man from Lilechem and put his son's spirit inside of him, placing the man's into the Yashel. Although his son is now in Jenoan form, he has the appearance of the young man. In his new form he is able to roam freely through Shonrar, Lilechem and Leychr. He remembers some of the body's previous memories and therefore can avoid Jenoans the man knew. For all the destruction he has caused to the inhabitants of the two cities (Lilechem and Shonrar), they have named him Darkness because he normally attacks after dark and nobody knows who it is killing Jenoans. Milo has been teaching Darkness some of his tricks and has managed to secure him with an illegal Hader of level four. The highest level anyone in Phosia has yet had.

Non-Birthday Birthday Party

Dan is hunting in the Shonrar forest when he thinks he sees something running through the trees. He goes to investigate but cannot see the creature. Dan returns to his apartment he shares with Alemap. On the way he sees Christian looking a bit shady.

Dan: "Christian, can I have a word?"

Christian: "Hi, yes, erm I just came to have a word with Alemap. Is she in?"

Dan: "I don't know, I'll check." He places his hand on the door to unlock it. "I wanted to talk to you about something I saw in the woods. I sensed it was, well…"

Christian: "In a minute, Dan." Dan switched the lights on and all his training colleagues and friends jumped out from behind furniture and walls. "Surprise" they all yelled. Alemap came over and gave him a kiss on the cheek. "Happy birthday" she said.

Dan: "Wow, thanks for being here everyone, this is such a surprise…"

Christian whispered in his ear "I blew it didn't I, When you saw me standing here?"

Dan: "Yes" he replied, "I'd forgotten all about my birthday…" he said to everyone. "Until I saw you acting strangely, that is", he whispered to Christian who smiled at himself hopelessly, saying "great" as he shook his head.

Alemap: "Are you alright?" she asked Christian.

Christian: "Yes, I'm fine, just being an idiot." Dan looked around the room. "Alemap, where's Mal?"

Alemap: "He should be along anytime he's just gone to

get your…" there was a knock at the door. "This should be him now." She pressed a button on the wall next to the door and the door disappeared until she took her hand off the switch. From the outside there was Mal. He was looking straight at the door, which from his point of view was still shut. She opened the door. Mal was holding a big cake in his hands. He entered the room and placed it on the table.

Mal: "Happy birthday."

Dan: "Well, it's more of an anniversary really. I can't even remember my real birthday. I think it was in November." Alemap went over to Julian and thanked him for the new security system on the door, which meant anyone could look out but no one could see in.

Mal: "Dan, come here. Everyone; this here is a cake Alemap and I found from researching Earth's cookery. Close your eyes and tell me how it tastes." Dan closed his eyes and Mal lifted the lid off the cake. Dan could hear Jenoans gasping. "Open wide" Mal said. "This is called a mud cake. Supposedly it is a delicacy on Earth." Dan was about to eat it when Mal added "and amongst marsh creatures." Dan instantly pulled away and opened his eyes.

Mal: "What's wrong?"

Alemap: "Are you allergic, like you were to the sauce I made you because I could whip up an antidote? I don't want you missing out. I know you said you liked this dessert."

Dan: "Dessert, erm, yes. It's not that I don't like it. Well, actually it is. The name 'Mud Cake', well that's all it is. We don't eat mud. It's just to describe how it looks. Mud cakes are actually made of chocolate. You know, that stuff I eat loads of."

Mal: "Oh. Well, I'm sure there are some marsh creatures who would love some of this right now." Everyone laughs. Dan returns from the food machine. "Now this is a 'Chocolate Mud Cake'. Everyone try some, I'll go make some more." He stood at the food machine waiting for a couple to be created and smiled to himself, because even though he couldn't be with his friends and family from home, he had made a new family and friends here.

Christian: "Now, as a celebration of Dan becoming twenty-one, we think, and because you have all done so well in your training, I thought we should all go to the beach tomorrow. It may be the last time before you all leave for college."

Dan: "You have a beach? How come I never knew about this? I love the beach, apart from sand getting everywhere."

The celebrations went on for a few hours and then most Jenoans left. Christian and Mal were the last to leave.

Dan: "Thank you, I had a brilliant time."

Mal: "My pleasure." They hug each other.

Alemap: "So we'll go to the beach after Dan gets his Hader updated tomorrow."

Christian: "That's fine. We'll be waiting in the feast hall." Bye Dan, happy birthday and congratulations.

Upgrade

The next morning Alemap woke to find a note from Dan telling her he was going for a swim. She was just about to go and find him when he appeared from the pool entrance to the apartment. This was a feature all the new apartments, which were built into the waterfall, had. The residents could get in using the hand register once to get into the facility from the pool outside, and then again to get into their room. Normally, an outside wall was in the up position allowing the Jenoans of Shonrar to go in and out this route as they pleased. It was put down at night time and during attacks. This meant that the waterfall would be spraying further out during the day with the wall up and then straight down at night. When the wall was down, access to the rooms was still available via the steps and paths behind the waterfall itself.

Alemap: "Hurry up and get dressed. It's time to go to have your Hader upgraded."

Dan: "OK, I won't be long. Do I have time for some breakfast?"

Alemap: "If you're quick."

After having breakfast and getting changed, Dan set off to the courtyard with Alemap, where a Jenoan technician from Lilechem was coming to upgrade his Hader. It turned out he was running late but with good reason.

Alemap: "Go to the hall with the others, I'll come to meet you there with the technician. Let Christian know. I don't want you setting off to the beach without me."

Dan: "OK, see you there." Dan set off for the hall where all the feasts were held. He was just out of calling range when Alemap spotted the technician running towards her. When he arrived he was very out of breath.

Alemap: "You're a little late so I've sent Dan along to the feast hall with his friends. We're all going to the beach today."

Technician: "No" he panted, "I've seen one, in the woods."

Alemap: "Seen what?"

Technician: "One of them. They're back."

Alemap: "One of what?" She paused for a second "no, you don't mean…?"

Technician: "A Leychrian!" She could tell by the look on his face he was not joking around.

Alemap: "Quick come with me. We must inform Christian." The technician, hardly having time to catch his breath, followed her to the hall. There she grabbed Christian as though she was about to throttle him and took him to one side. "We need to talk."

The boys looked on as the two of them talked, Alemap getting more frustrated and Christian's face dropping to the floor as her friend, who had by now caught his breath, explained what he had seen.

James: "Go on Dan; ask them what's going on."

Dan: "Why me? You're his son Matthew, why don't you go?"

Matthew: "Because you're the favourite."

Ryan & Corey: "Because you're the 'Chosen One'."

Dan: "Shut up." Dan always took their jokes with a pinch of salt because he didn't see himself as being better than any of them. He did what they asked and questioned what was going on. Christian wasn't going to say anything but Alemap insisted, in a way only she could.

Dan: "Yes, that's right. That's what I was going to tell you yesterday before my party. I had a bad feeling and then I saw something that I thought could be a Leychrian."

Alemap: "Why didn't you tell us?"

Dan: "Party. It kind of slipped my mind." He turned to the technician. "I'm sorry, I didn't catch your name."

Technician: "It's Taylor."

Dan: "Now Taylor, how positive are you it was a Leychrian?"

Taylor: "About ninety percent sure."

Dan: "Me too" he said with a sigh.

Christian: "Right, Alemap and I will contact Lilechem see if they've heard anything. The guards posted at Leychr might have seen something. Can you contact them?" She nodded. He turned to Dan, "You lot wait here and we'll be back once we have news." He addressed the other boys, "Sorry, but the trip's going to be postponed for a while." They moaned and watched them walk out.

Mission Falcon

Taylor was left standing not knowing whom to follow. Dan turned to him took off his Hader and threw it to him.

Dan:	"How long is it going to take you to upgrade that thing?"
Taylor:	"About twenty minutes."
Dan:	"OK, then get started." He walked over to the others. "Right this is what's happening." He told them the situation. When he had finished, they were discussing what they were going to do when Dan had a thought. "Hold on a second." He went over to Taylor.
Taylor:	"It's going to take me another ten minutes, I can't work any faster."
Dan:	"No, it's not that, but thanks for this anyway. I was wondering which way was the… …thing, shall we say, heading?"
Taylor:	"Towards the Sandy Mountains."
Dan:	"Thanks." He went back to the group. "OK, the thing was heading towards Leychr when I saw it yesterday and today it's heading towards the Sandy Mountains. That would have given it enough time to see what's going on in Leychr."
Jake:	"So it was a scout for the returning Leychrians?"
Graeme:	"Possibly, but where have they been hiding; in

the Sandy Mountains?"

Matthew: "Why, it's not very habitable for their kind."

Graeme: "Yes, but there's no way that thousands of Leychrians passed through the Shonrar forest undetected. It's like they vanished. I would have thought they would be in the Snowy Mountains."

Ben: "Yes, they could have easily got up there without anyone seeing them and how did they know about the attack anyway?"

Jordan: "So what are we going to do?"

Dan: "Well, that guy will have followed the road here from Lilechem so if we hurry, we could still cut the thing off before it heads up the mountain."

Mal: "If that's where it's really going."

Jordan: "Well we don't have many choices, so I say we go with that idea and see where it takes us."

Taylor: "I've finished." They all start walking towards him, which is a little intimidating to him. "You're on level four now but I will need to check it is alright in a few hours and if so, I can just initialise the permanent upgrade."

Dan: "Thanks. Right boys lets get some weapons and head out."

Mal: "If anyone asks, we've headed off for the beach and will meet them there if they are coming. If not they can contact us on our Haders."

Taylor: "What shall I do?"

Mal: "Stay there, they should be back soon."

James: "Help yourself to food from the back there." He pointed to where they kept the food and the technician went over to it without haste. Outside, Dan and the boys picked up their weapons from the stables. Dan put his Hader back on. "Aw, I'd forgotten how much these sting when you first put them on."

Corey: "So you're up to a level four now. Even Christian only has a level three."

Ben: "I think Lord Stephen has a four."

Jordan: "Yes, don't they give them to all Lords of Phosia?" No one knew the answer for sure.

Ryan: "So what extra features does it have now?"

Dan: "I don't know, normally Alemap or someone tells me. Or I just find out when I need it and it automatically happens. Everyone ready? Right then, we may as well take some griffins. It will cut time off our journey."

The Leychrian & The Boy

The boys rode towards the Sandy Mountains at top speed, in an attempt to capture the creature. As they got nearer to their estimated point of merger Dan's Hader activated itself, alarming his griffin, which nearly threw him off. He halted the rest of the group and they all watched as his Hader showed the outline of a creature coming towards them. They were all quite excited that they could see the creature's image - the upgrade provided a holographic projection from the Hader screen and it was this that had spooked the griffin when it just suddenly came on.

Dan: "How do I get this onto silent mode? If we tie the griffins up here and then move on by foot, we can surround it before it leaves the trees." The boys did as Dan suggested and hid in the trees and foliage waiting for the beast to arrive. Dan watched on his Hader, but suddenly got down out of the tree he was waiting in. Mal climbed down from the tree next to him.

Mal: "What's wrong?"

Dan: "I don't know, but I suddenly feel sick." He was grasping his stomach for a few seconds when Jordan who was in a bush near Dan noticed another being pop up on the image created by his Hader.

Jordan: "Look, something else is there, in front of it."

Dan: "Yes and it's evil, it's really evil." As quickly as the pain had started, it subsided. The boys looked to the Hader, which showed the creature, thought to be a Leychrian, run into the path of the other unknown being who was stationary.

Dan began reading the information the Hader was telling him "They're in a clearing two miles from here, come on let's go."

The Clearing

Darkness appeared before the only Leychrian seen in the Shonrar woods for several years. He was rubbing his head when the Leychrian passed by, not noticing him.

Darkness: "What are you doing scout, you're about to be caught by Jenoans and him? I can sense him coming for us."

Scout: "What do we do?"

Darkness: "We leave." Darkness grabs hold of the Leychrian and they disappear from Dan's Hader.

Dan: "They're gone."

Matthew: "But where, they didn't pass us."

Corey: "Perhaps your Hader's malfunctioning?"

Dan: "I don't think so."

Graeme: "What was that thing?"

Dan: "I'm not sure, but even though it was definitely evil I could feel something familiar about it."

Ben: "How do you mean?"

Dan: "I'm not sure."

Jake: "I think we should be getting back now. They've probably realised we're not there anymore." No sooner had Jake said it Dan's Hader activated itself and Christian's face appeared before them.

Christian: "Get back here now…" Alemap pushed him out of the way to get to the screen "Dan, where are you? Get back here immediately."

Dan: "OK, we're on our way."

Ryan: "I think they know were not at the beach."

Dan: "Erm, yes. Let's go find the griffins. Where were we when we left them?" Once again the Hader came on and this time an Arrow appeared pointing the way back to the animals. "I need to get an on/off switch with this thing." They headed back to the griffins.

Milo's Cave

Darkness brought the scout back to his father's cave, where Milo was trying to figure out how to use the Shafellor crystal.

Milo: "So what have you found out?" He said placing the crystal down.

Scout: "There are only a handful of guards in Leychr.

	It will be easy to sneak up on them from the inside."
Milo:	"How long before they are ready to do that?"
Scout:	"The tunnels are still blocked from the cave in when we arrived here, I do not know how long it will be before they are finished."
Milo:	"Go tell Rechly I want to see him."
Scout:	"Yes, right away." He turned to leave, but Darkness took him by the throat and lifted him in the air. "Aren't we forgetting something?"
Scout:	"No, I don't think so."
Darkness:	"Yes, right away… what?"
Scout:	"Yes, right away … Master? Yes, right away Master." Darkness dropped him and he scurried away to find Rechly.
Darkness:	"We work with such idiots. He nearly let himself get captured."
Milo:	"By Lilechem or Shonrar?"
Darkness:	"Shonrar, and even worse, it was him and his little swarm of ants who were about to discover it, not Christian or the other leaders."
Milo:	"Don't worry. Soon enough Dan will be coming here looking for something. Things have already been set in motion and then we shall use him to steal back my sceptre and betray his new family, before we kill him. Or even better; watch them do it for us. The ending doesn't really matter and then we can restore you back to your old self by taking back what he stole from you."
Darkness:	"I want to kill him; the way he killed me."
Milo:	"Ah yes, death by fire. Although that's pretty

quick, you should torture him first."

Darkness: "OK, when do we lure him here?"

Milo: "We don't. He'll come of his own accord and then…"

Darkness: "Then what?"

Milo: "…we shall have him in our clutches."

Shonrar Hall

The group arrive back from their trip. Alemap and Christian are waiting for them.

Dan: "They don't look too happy."

Mal: "No, not at all."

Dan: "Oh well, we'll be leaving for college in a few days. They can't do anything too bad, can they?" As they put their griffins into the stable and take off their weapons Alemap comes over to Dan. "Are you done?"

Dan: "Yes."

Alemap: "Come with me then."

Dan: "Where are we going?"

Alemap: "We're off to see Lord Stephen. He wants a word with you. The rest of you finish up here and go over to Christian."

Ben: "Do you think because he's the 'Chosen One' he gets a harsher telling off?"

Jordan: "He probably gets whipped into shape. That's why he's always such a goodie, goodie." Christian called to them from outside the stables. "You lot, get out here now." The two boys rolled their eyes at each other and headed out with the others to the courtyard.

Task 3

In the hall, Dan was getting his stern telling off from Alemap. As they got nearer to Lord Stephen, Alemap's voice got quieter, but was still quite forceful. Lord Stephen was sitting on the front of the platform that had been erected for performances and for the leaders table when feasting. He asked Dan to sit by him. Alemap stood close by leaning on a table.

Lord Stephen: "Do you know why I have brought you here today Dan?"

Dan: "To shout at me for what I did today?"

Lord Stephen: "No. I'm only a few years your senior, I would not presume to shout at you as a parent would." He paused for a second. "Why, what did you do? You didn't blow anything up did you?"

Dan: "No, nothing like that, I…"

Lord Stephen: "It's probably best I don't know, if it doesn't concern me or Shonrar."

Dan: "What do you need me for then?"

Lord Stephen: "It is time for your final test. Do you think you're ready?"

Dan: "As ready as I'm going to be; I've done all my training and everything. I have my new Hader, although it would be good if I had learned how to work it first."

Lord Stephen: "That comes with time. You still have all the features you already use and a few added extras." Dan grew sad as he realised something. "What's wrong?"

Dan: "If I do this, does this mean I'll be going home?"

Alemap: "You've got to survive it first." The other two looked at her. She grinned and said "Joke!"

Lord Stephen: "Don't you want to go home? You can stay here if you would like. You know you'll always be welcome here."

Alemap: "And you could always change your mind when the mirror recharges."

Dan: "Well, I have my life here now and my friends, and my new family," he said looking up at Alemap, who blushed. "I do miss my family but they must think I'm dead. They will have moved on with their lives and I think if I go back after all these years it would be too painful for them." Tears were in his eyes as he thought about his family. "And I'm just going to start college. What would Mal do without me? I know all of us get on, but we've been partners for a long time, ever since his Dad died."

Lord Stephen: "That is something you can think about later. For now, you should concentrate on the task. You can't let these things cloud your judgement right now. Besides, if you survive, which I'm positive you will, then there is still the battle to be won. These things don't happen overnight, so you could be with us for a bit longer yet."

Dan: "What do I have to do? I'm ready."

Alemap: "I'm going to go outside for a minute."

Lord Stephen: "You can stay this time if you like."

Alemap: "No, it's alright." she said. "Dan, come here and give me a hug before you go." He did. As he was going to sit back down and with his back turned to her she pointed at Dan and re-enacted a moment from the past. Lord Stephen nodded at her.

Lord Stephen: "So, it has been a long time coming, but it is finally time for your last task before the battle."

Dan: "Wouldn't you call the battle the final task? It's just another thing I have to survive."

Lord Stephen: "I suppose you could do, but a battle and a task are two very different things. So far, you have only had to keep yourself alive."

Dan: "And that girl, Tyra, I saved in the Snowy Mountains. I should have gone back really and let her know I'm still alive. I don't want her hating those dragons for killing me. They were so nice."

Falcon's Punishment

Outside Christian has got the boys to muck out the griffin stables. Alemap approaches him. "So how's it going?" he asks.

Alemap: "They're in there now, having the talk."

Christian: "What about? His last task?"

Alemap: "That and the talk."

Christian: "The talk? Oh, you mean the whole fiery death thing. That can't be easy. He's a good kid though. As long as we tell him the circumstances in which it happened, I'm sure he'll understand."

Alemap: "He's had it tough though; being away from his family for so long. I know we're only a substitute but I do think of him as a son to me."

Christian: "Yes, but substitute or not, it's not like the ones he has back on Earth are his real parents either."

The Tasks Description

Lord Stephen: "Are we going to get on to your task."

Dan: "Yes, sorry."

Lord Stephen: "This maybe your hardest task, but it is the simplest to explain. You need to go to the Snowy Mountains and find Milo's cave. In there, he has a purple crystal. Bring it back to us." Dan sat there for a moment waiting for some more.

Dan: "Is that it?"

Lord Stephen: "That's what the prophecy says and then you should receive a weapon to help us win the battle ahead."

Dan: "So all I have to do is find this crystal and bring it back to you and then I shall receive a weapon, from you?"

Lord Stephen: "I don't know exactly how these things work. We just give you the information we have and then things tend to work out as it says. You will win us the battle. This time we can make it easier on you. Take whoever you want to find Milo."

Dan: "I think I have a good idea where he is and it's not in the Snowy Mountains."

Lord Stephen: "Excellent, that helps a great deal. If not, you have your Hader to help you track, alongside your inexplicable talent for sensing danger. It is very useful having a human around with that kind of talent."

Dan: "I don't think it's a human thing. I can't remember my parents or anyone else I knew being able to do it. Then again, we didn't have to hunt for our food. We just went down the local supermarket. I have had all that training as well, which will have helped."

Lord Stephen: "You certainly surpass any Jenoan I've ever met."

Dan: "Thank you. I suppose I'd better be going then."

Lord Stephen: "Well, good luck. You have my full support to do whatever is necessary to complete your task and win this battle. Don't forget you can contact us from anywhere in Phosia using your Hader, if you need anything."

Dan: "It's just a shame that it comes on when it wants. It would be better if it didn't when I need to be sneaking around."

Lord Stephen: "Just put it in stealth mode. Just think 'stealth mode' and it will give you a tingling sensation in your arm when it wants to activate something. Look at the screen, it will tell you what it wants to do and then you can OK it if you want; just think it. Oh and to get it back to normal just think 'normal mode'."

Dan: "Thanks, that's good to know. By the way you keep mentioning a big battle?"

Lord Stephen: "Well, it says in the prophecy that this will be the first big battle once you have succeeded in your task and you will be able to help us with the weapon you acquire."

Dan: "So I have to help you in all these battles before I can go home?"

Lord Stephen: "No, it just says about this battle. After that we'll use the weapon to protect ourselves."

Dan: "And what if I don't do this task? Will that not prevent the battles in the first place?"

Lord Stephen: "The battles will probably go on with or without you doing the task, but if you do and you succeed, at least we will have the resources to defend ourselves." He heads for the door. Alemap is coming back towards them when Lord Stephen remembers her skit.

Lord Stephen: "Oh and Dan, Alemap wants me to remind you that you could still die. Don't be cocky, Milo is a powerful guy, you will need to be cunning and play him at his own tricks if necessary."

Dan: "OK, see you soon then... hopefully." He rolls his eyes at Alemap as she walks past him in the entrance.

Conspiracy

Alemap walks back into the room and sits by Lord Stephen. With a worried look on her face, she asks, "How did he take it?"

Lord Stephen: "He's a smart boy. He'll cope and at least he's not alone in it this time."

Alemap: "Yes, but I didn't think he'd want us helping him if he found out that we're the reason he killed that young boy to bring him here."

Lord Stephen: "You haven't told him about that yet? He's been here fourteen years. No wonder he's such a well adjusted kid if he's still in the dark."

Alemap: "You mean, you didn't just tell him?" She rose to her feet. "What about me giving you the whole..." she redid the little skit.

Lord Stephen: "I thought you were portraying death and you wanted me to remind him he may not come back. Quickly, go after him! He can't find out from someone else, it would crush him." Alemap runs outside after Dan, who is apologising to Christian.

Alemap: "Dan, can we have a talk before you go off."

Dan: "Yes, of course. See you when I get back", he says to Christian. The two of them begin walking off towards the apartment. Mal looks on at them as they walk away.

Alemap: "There's something I've been meaning to tell you for a long time now and it's not something that's easy for me to say, so I'll just say it because you need to know before you leave and you should have been told a long time ago. I thought Lord Stephen was telling you then, but obviously not, so I'll have to tell you…"

Across the courtyard Mal has stopped work and was lost in thought.

Christian: "You can find out what Lord Stephen had to say later. As for now get back to work."

Mal: "Sorry Christian" he replied. He glanced over one last time and put his head down, but put it straight back up when he realised he had seen Dan doubled over, holding his stomach.

Alemap: "What's wrong?" Dan didn't reply in words but groans of pain. Then suddenly it stopped. He stood up.

Dan: "Well, at least that wasn't as bad as the first one."

Alemap: "You've had this pain before?"

Dan: "Yes, once before, in the woods." Dan then sensed a presence in the woods behind them.

Alemap: "Come back to the apartment and I'll have a look at you."

Dan: "No, it's alright now. The pain goes away instantly when it stops."

Alemap: "Still, I'd rather make sure it's not something serious."

Dan: "OK, I'll be there soon and then we can talk. There's something I have to do first."

Alemap heads back to the apartment while Dan goes out towards the woods. From the stable he is in, Mal can see a figure standing near the entrance to Shonrar in the woods. The figure walks into the woods and Dan follows him.

Mal: "Christian."

Christian: "Yes."

Mal: "Dan's gone into the woods alone."

Christian: "He has his final task to do. Hmm, that must mean the battle will be soon. OK, that's enough for today. Get yourselves cleaned up and we'll do some training."

Dan & Darkness

Dan walked out of the courtyard and followed the figure into the Shonrar woods. They had been walking for about five minutes, when Dan decided to run to catch up with it. As he set off running, the figure disappeared into nowhere. Dan walked to the spot where the figure was, but could not find a trace of it.

He looked around not knowing which way to go. "Hello? Where are you?" There was no reply. The pain in Dan's stomach came back but this time only lasted a couple of seconds. "I know you're here. I can sense you." He followed his instincts to where he though it could be. His Hader was activated in stealth mode so he looked down at it wrapped around his wrist. It wanted to display the location of something near him but Dan didn't need it. As soon as he had thought this, the feeling in his arm subsided and the Hader deactivated itself. "What do you want?" Dan shouted as he proceeded through the woods. "Why won't you talk to me? Can you talk?" he walked a little way further and then sensed that it had stopped. Dan began running towards it.

Dan had reached the lake in the middle of the Shonrar woods, which was also known as the Oasis. In a clearing up ahead, a Jenoan stood with his back to Dan. When he reached him he started walking away again. "Wait!" Dan shouted. The figure stopped in his tracks and turned round to face Dan. He was wearing a robe with the hood covering his face. "Finally! You're quite hard to keep up with. So what's this all about? Who are you?"

Darkness: "They call me Darkness." He pulled the hood off his face. Dan drew his sword. "I see you've heard of me then."

Dan: “Oh, I’ve heard of you and about all the Jenoans you’ve murdered.”

Darkness: “They had it coming.” He said with a smile.

Dan: “What possible excuse could you have to justify the murder of innocent Jenoans?”

Darkness began to get agitated “My excuse is that they killed me and now it’s their turn.”

Dan: “If they murdered you, then how are you standing here?”

Darkness: “My father brought me back.”

Dan: “Your father? What is he, some kind of God?”

Darkness: “He is Milo.”

Dan: “Milo?”

Darkness: “Oh so you don’t know then.”

Dan: “Know what?”

Darkness: “Your relationship with me and why I hate you and your kind so much.”

Dan: “Hate me, how can you hate me? I’ve never even met you before.”

Darkness: “Not true. We’ve met on several occasions; the first time was fourteen years ago when you killed me.”

Dan: “What are you talking about?” Darkness drew a sword and ran at Dan. They had a short fight but were equally matched, each sensing the others moves before they could strike.

Darkness: “We’re getting nowhere and I can’t kill you right now, because my father is expecting you.” He whispered under his breath, “He never said in how many pieces though." Darkness turned around and threw his sword at Dan, who just stopped it from hitting him before it plunged into a tree trunk. "We will finish this later, you and I, but for now you have a rendezvous with Milo. Don't disappoint him if you want to know more." He held out his hand and the sword flew out of the tree and landed in his hands. Darkness ran off into the woods. Dan followed him but he disappeared again and Dan couldn't sense him anymore.

For a few minutes he stood confused as to what Darkness was saying. He didn't know him, so he knew he could be lying but couldn't work out what he would have to gain from it.

His Hader activated. Alemap was calling him. He was about to answer but then changed his mind and headed for the Sandy Mountains.

Alemap's Apartment

Back in Shonrar, Alemap was frantic worrying about Dan. Christian and Lord Stephen were with her in her apartment. "Why hasn't he come back and why is he not answering his Hader?"

Lord Stephen: "He's probably begun the task already. He may not be in a position to get in touch with us yet."

Christian: "He will do when he can."

Alemap: "What if he's dead? He must be…that's why he's not answering!"

Lord Stephen: "That's not possible. If he was dead, then the Hader would stop itself functioning and we would be informed. Just like if he takes it off and it's not being powered by his biological system."

Christian: "What if he's taken it off or lost it?"

Lord Stephen: "Possible; he could have taken it off, but he couldn't have lost it. Unless his arm was chopped off." Alemap whined. "Then again, the Hader would still be active until someone else picked it up or Dan left without it."

Christian: "Then what?"

Lord Stephen: "Same again, it would deactivate itself."

Christian: "So even if it does get reported as being deactivated, Dan could still be alive." He said, trying to comfort Alemap.

Alemap: "Yes, but he wouldn't have an arm then." She cries on Lord Stephen's shoulder.

Christian: "But at least he wouldn't be dead." Lord Stephen stops him there before he says anything else. "I'm going back to train the boys. I'll come back later, see how you are."

Dan Finds Out The Truth

Dan headed to the top of the Sandy Mountains. From there, he could see over the top of the Shonrar woods. It was a clear sky and still light. Dan could make out Leychr and the Snowy Mountains in the distance. He walked on until he was level with Leychr. His Hader activated, as he had a vision of the past. He was looking down at Leychr from the Snowy Mountains when he saw the light from a cave somewhere across from the corridor that led to the room where Maddox died. He snapped out of his vision and used his Hader to zoom in on Leychr. He located the tower where the corridor would be behind and then the Hader pinpointed the approximate position of the cave. "Huh! That's clever! Show me the way then." Dan looked down at his Hader and an arrow appeared, guiding the way to the cave.

In Milo's cave, Milo was talking with Rechly. Darkness was

standing outside, trying to sense Dan. When he did, he came back inside. “He’s coming.”

Milo: “How near?”

Darkness: “From the position he’s coming from, he’ll see Rechly if he leaves now.”

Milo: “Right then, both of you go down through the back.” Darkness pointed the way for Rechly. He followed him into the back, but scowled at him when he wasn’t looking. Milo chuckled to himself.

Dan entered the cave. “Welcome, I’ve been expecting you. Do you know why you’re here?”

Dan: “Why do you think I’m here?”

Milo: “It’s your final task. You have come to take something from me. Can you see what it is you require?” Dan looks around the room and sees the purple crystal displayed in a cabinet, along with other treasures Milo had stolen from the Temple in the Snowy Mountains. “Do you think you can?”

Dan was about to say he knew he could, when he remembered what Lord Stephen had said about not being cocky. When he had finished this thought with the use of his Hader, Dan replied “Maybe.” Dan’s thought, could not be seen by Milo and he didn’t even realise Dan’s mind was temporarily somewhere else.

Milo: “That’s not the only reason though is it?”

Dan: “What do you mean?”

Milo: “Well, it’s such a simple task. Steal something from me and then use it to make your weapon to destroy me. The reason you’re here is to learn a few things. But the question is why did you come alone?"

Dan: "It's my task; I didn't want to endanger anyone else."

Milo: "Ha, ha! That's very noble of you, but you endanger your little friends' everyday. Taking them out after that Leychrian when you knew you should have asked permission."

Rechly and Darkness are listening in. When Rechly hears Milo blow the Leychrians cover, he goes to step out and confront him and kill Dan.

Rechly: "He's just confirmed to him that we're back." Darkness grabs hold of him, stares him in the face and says, "He knows what he is doing." He then throws him back into the back room.

Dan glances at his Hader to see the shapes of a Jenoan man and a Leychrian fighting.

Milo: "That will be my son, Darkness. I believe you've met him."

Dan: "Yes. I've had the pleasure today."

Milo: "And before. He was the one who retrieved the Leychrian for me, when you risked you friend's lives to go out and capture it alone."

Dan: "We can handle ourselves; we don't need supervising all the time."

Milo: "That maybe true of you, but can the same be said about the rest?"

Dan: "Each one of them is extremely talented. We may not have the years of experience that Christian and the other leaders do, but we're the best young trainees in Shonrar and Lilechem." He then shuts up thinking about his cockiness again.

Milo: "That maybe, but you, you're different to the rest. You know that."

Dan: "Well I'm not from this planet, so I guess I must have some advantage from that."

Milo: "You don't know anything do you? You have these special abilities over the rest of them; best of all you broke that little present for me all those years ago in Leychr. Three of you were exposed to it, otherwise you would have been invulnerable now."

Dan: "So the whole sensing danger thing? That's from the glowy light thing."

Milo: "Well done! You're starting to put the pieces together again now."

Dan: "So who was the third? Only me and Teburnt were in the room… and that floating thing that went after the glowy light thing."

Milo: "You mean Darkness."

Dan: "Darkness? Him?" he said pointing to the other room. "Why was he a floating thing?"

Milo: "Because he was dead. That was his spirit, his soul, his essence if you will."

Dan: "And now?"

Milo: "Oh now he's very much alive; as you can hear." Dan glanced back down at his Hader to see the two still fighting in the back.

Milo: "Clever thing that Hader. I bet you're seeing two body signatures in there right now."

Dan: "I don't know what you're talking about."

Milo: "If you know what you're doing, you can use it to see so much more."

Dan: "I killed him."

Milo: "What?"

Dan: "I killed him, Darkness. That's what he said."

Milo: "You did."

Dan: "I don't understand, how? When?"

Milo: "You're really kept in the dark about all the important issues aren't you? Yes, you killed him when you arrived in this world. In order for you to get here without a Hader, my son was used as a sacrifice." His tone begins to get angry, yet he is looking at the floor as he is speaking. "They put him on that altar and left him to die slowly. He had the life force sucked out of him to initialise the flame to find you. He was strung up against his will and held there until you arrive in your flame and finally burned the altar, and him, to the ground, ensuring your essence is held here in Phosia." The two of them were both tearful. "He was a bright young boy. He even used to play with Mal and the rest of them when he was younger." He began getting angry again, "If it wasn't for these stupid prophecies, he would be alive now and off to college."

Dan: "But he is alive now."

Milo: "Yes, but in someone else's body. It's just a host with his essence within it. Who knows what he could have grown up to do, to become? Think of all the Jenoans who have been killed so he can live, and all because of you."

Dan: "I'm sorry. I don't know what I can say, I…" Darkness came out of the back.

Darkness: "There's nothing you can say or do to put me back as I was. I have to live my life as someone else and because of you and my father, I have become a murderer in order to live again."

Dan: "That's why you've killed all these Jenoans?"

Milo: "Don't get us wrong, we would have only killed those who had any involvement in bringing you here, but we had no way of telling who had the right attributes."

Darkness: "You're lucky your precious Alemap is so well protected, otherwise we could have used her to do what we needed."

Milo: "Maddox was a good donor though. We used his essence to help hold Darkness in the host's body, but it won't last."

Dan: "So you'll have to kill again?"

Darkness: "Yes. Why? Got anyone in mind you'd like us to sacrifice?"

Dan: "Just one."

Darkness: "Please be Alemap."

Dan: "Not Alemap, me."

Who's The Stranger?

In Shonrar, everyone is worried about how long Dan is taking to get in contact. They believe he may have been captured.

Alemap: "What can we do? We can't just sit here waiting. We should be out there looking for him."

Christian: "We don't even know where he's gone."

Alemap: "We could track him using his Hader. You know, pin point his position and then go after him."

Lord Stephen: "No you can't. Not if he has it in stealth mode, which he did when he left. He wouldn't know to put it back on normal mode himself for that reason."

Christian: "Do you know where he is Lord Stephen?"

Lord Stephen: "I know he's gone to find Milo's hiding place and that he had a good idea where it might be."

Alemap: "So what are we waiting for? We should go now."

Lord Stephen: "He didn't tell me where it was; just that he had a fair idea."

Alemap: "So you're saying all we can do is wait here and do nothing?"

Lord Stephen: "If he needs us, he will contact us. What about this figure Christian, who could he have been following?"

Christian: "I don't know, Mal just said he saw him walking towards someone but they were hiding under a hood. It doesn't sound like anyone he'd know from the village that I can think of. Dan would normally just get into trouble with the rest of his training unit."

Lord Stephen: "Could it be someone from one of your other groups?"

Christian: "I don't know, without having a proper description, it could be anyone."

Lord Stephen: "All we can do now is pray that he is safe and that he returns to us soon."

Christian: "And with the weapon."

Offering

In Milo's cave Dan has offered himself in the place of someone else. Milo has accepted his offer and Dan goes outside to think.

Milo: "I was hoping you'd want to be a willing participant in Darkness' rebirth. Don't worry. You won't feel any pain. I'm not heartless. You didn't know what you were coming to and in a way you're not to blame. However, you are standing here right now and if all goes to plan you will be the one who allows Darkness to stay Jenoan permanently."

Dan: "So you won't need to kill anymore of the others."

Milo: "No, if it is permanent then I won't need any others for revenge. I will have my son back. True, I would like my old life back and not to be banished from the land where I was born, but there are plenty of other worlds we can go to. Once he is whole again, that is."

Dan: "What do I have to do?"

Milo: "This way." Milo takes Dan back into the cave where he uncovers a crystal behind some curtains.

Dan: "What's that?"

Milo: "That is what I'm going to use to drain your essence from you; the Yashel Crystal. Darkness" he shouts, "Come here." Darkness comes leaving Rechly watching from a distance. He can only see the back of Dan's head and not his face or any other identifiable features.

As Dan enters the room with the Yashel Crystal, he has an overwhelming feeling come over him, pulling him to the crystal.

Milo: "Don't be afraid boy. It won't hurt you, much."

Milo instructs Dan to stand at one side of the crystal and Darkness at the other. As Dan looks into the crystal, it starts to glow with four different sequences of colours, swirling around inside. There are reds, yellows and orange followed by blues and green. In the third sequence there are browns and greens and finally whites and blues. Milo snaps his fingers in front of Dan's face to bring him back from the trance he seems to be in.

Milo: "Yes, it is very interesting but we have something to be getting on with, don't we."

Dan: "What shall I do?"

Milo: "Hold your hands out, a little in front of the crystal and then Darkness will do the rest."

Dan does as Milo asks. Darkness places his hands on the Yashel Crystal and says, "Come to me."

The crystal changes from colourful swirls to black and Dan's essence start to leave his body from his hands, passing through the crystal and entering into Darkness.

The Plot

After a few minutes Milo takes some cloth and throws it over the Yashel Crystal. Dan feels very drained; Milo helps him to sit down. "Here we go. You rest now, that will have taken a lot out of you." Darkness though, feeling energised, scowls at his father's behaviour towards their enemy.

Milo: "You just rest up there. I'll get you something to eat and drink. You need to keep your strength up for next time. Darkness, come and help me." He signals with his eyes, telling Darkness to follow him. They leave the room and head into the back where Rechly is still hiding and observing.

Rechly: "What's taking so long?" They walk passed him.

Darkness: "Shut up." He turns to his father. "What the hell was that?"

Milo: "Keep your voice down." He demands sternly. In a slightly lowered speaking voice they continue their argument.

Darkness: "Why is he still alive? I thought it was supposed to kill him."

Milo: "It is."

Darkness: "So why is he still here and why was it taking so long?"

Milo: "Listen, calm down. The reason it was taking so long is because we are using a live body now. He will have been resisting the transfer. His body anchors his essence within him when he's alive. When he's dead the spirit is freed."

Rechly: "So why don't we kill him now, then I can have a snack once you have finished with the body?"

Milo: "Shut up Rechly. We aren't going to kill him."

Darkness: "What?" he shouts. Milo shushes him.

Milo: "At least not today. We don't know whether the transfer will be permanent yet. If we leave it the usual time and you don't end up back in the Yashel then we can assume it has worked. Otherwise if we keep him alive we can continually use him to fill you up when you need it."

Darkness: "So what now?"

Milo: "When he's recovered, we can use him to do some tasks for us, like getting back my sceptre for a start and a few other things. Just be glad, you've had about enough now to restore you into your old body", he said, looking down where a sheet was laid on the floor. Milo and Darkness smiled at each other.

Rechly: "What, am I not in on the joke?"

Milo: "Look under the sheet." He lifts it up to uncover the remains of two skeletons, one an adult and one a child.

Rechly: "I don't understand?"

Darkness: "Those are my bones, they still hold my genetic code in them. Right father?"

Milo: "Exactly."

Rechly: "And the other?"

Darkness: "It's..." Milo shakes his head and he stops talking. They cover the skeletons back up.

Rechly: "But why would he help us? We've just tried to kill him, well you have, but he knows I'll eat him given half the chance." Darkness's host's Hader has activated showing Dan's figure coming near to the door. Milo holds his sons arm up so they can watch his movements. He shushes them both again. The Hader hadn't worked when Darkness brought the host's body to the cave but Milo managed to get around that problem with a few modifications. Dan walks over to the entrance to the tunnel that leads down into another room. He stands at the top of the tunnel, propping himself up on the wall staring at the scars on his hands, where his essence had left his body. Milo continued, aware that Dan was able to hear them.

Milo: "He trusts us now. He has no choice. We may be out to kill him eventually, but he knows we need him right now. And we haven't betrayed him. We've been honest about our intentions from the start. Whereas the Jenoans he's grown up with, teaching and disciplining him have lied to him his whole Phosian life. He can trust us because we need him, just as much as he needs us." They watched as Dan hobbled back to where he was sitting.

Milo: "See, now he believes we are his only friends and we can use that to our advantage. He's back round the corner. He won't be able to see you from where he's sitting, if you hurry out of here. Tell your troops that soon they can claim back their home and much more. Make sure all the digging is finished but don't get caught out. Kill any guards that maybe protecting the tunnels. I doubt they will have even found it, but if so, we can't let them inform Shonrar or Lilechem of our arrival. Go." Rechly scurries out of the cave on all fours and heads back into the Sandy Mountains.

Darkness: "So what now?"

Milo: "We give them what they've been wanting."

Darkness: "Which is?"

Milo: "The weapon to destroy us."

Darkness: "What, but they'll use it against us."

Milo: "They could, if they knew how to use it." He starts preparing some food and drink. "Besides, we won't give it to him straight away. First we'll get him to bring back the sceptre in two night's time. I can use that instantly, so we'll already have an advantage. Then we will know how you're holding up and whether you need another boost. After that we send him back with whatever it is in there that he needs to make a weapon."

Darkness: "I still don't see why you're giving him the weapon."

Milo: "Because then he'll go back to them and they'll believe they're winning, but we'll already be on the way to stop them with our army. They won't know what's hit them and then he can watch while they all die together. Then, it's his turn and I know you've been looking forward to that."

Darkness: "So until then I have to play nice?"

Milo: "You don't, but I do, just for a while. You know my loyalties are with you." Milo kisses Darkness on the forehead and they head into the other room. "Sorry about the wait, but we don't have any cooking machinery here, it all has to be prepared by hand. We have to do things the hard way in exile." Dan eats the food prepared for him while he listens to a very watered down version of what is going to happen.

After a couple of hours, having been bandaged up by Milo, Dan is sent back to Shonrar to retrieve the Sceptre for him, while Milo and Darkness just have to wait.

Shonrar

The Lake

In the middle of the Shonrar woods was the Oasis. Dan headed there from the Sandy Mountains. He didn't want anyone else to know where he had come from, so he headed there first. Before Dan had left, Milo had insisted that his Hader be altered so that he could see and hear everything that happened, just in case Dan was thinking of letting anybody else know what they had been up to. Dan sat on the bank of the lake thinking for a couple of hours. He needed some time to process what had happened to him. The truth about how he came to be in Phosia, the harsh reality about the lies told to him by his once trusted colleagues and the task set on him by Milo and Darkness. As he sat there, he dangled his feet over the bank and looked at his hands. When he looked up he saw something moving through the trees. He didn't know if he could trust his Hader given that Milo had tampered with it. He went to draw his sword, when out of the woods a unicorn came to drink on the opposite side of the lake. It had a shiny white coat and a golden horn. Dan put his sword away and watched as the magnificent creature lapped up the water. When it had finished, it looked at Dan and spoke to him with its mind. Dan was shocked for a moment when the voice came in his head, but after the dragons he half expected it.

Unicorn: "Don't be afraid. I won't hurt you." Dan spoke with his thoughts.

Dan: "Strange, that's normally what we say to animals like you. Not that we get a lot of animals like you, we have horses that are similar but without the whole golden horn on the forehead. I wonder if he knows what a horse is?"

Unicorn: "Settle down. I can hear all your thoughts. If you want to communicate with an animal of telepathic abilities, think as normal, but force the thoughts you want me to hear out of your head. Oh and aim them for me, unless you want anyone else telepathic to hear."

Dan: "How do I force them out?"

Unicorn: "Just concentrate harder on the words you want to say when talking to me. After a while, your regular thoughts are unheard by us, as you learn to focus the selected thoughts."

Dan: "Can I talk to you?" He spoke out loud.

Unicorn: "Don't speak it, think it. We don't want 'You Know Who' to listen in."

Dan: "Sorry" he thought forcefully.

Unicorn: "That's it. The thoughts you force take precedence when communicating and other thoughts get drowned out. Besides, I have no idea what you said in your native tongue. While wearing your Hader we can understand each other. It doesn't work when you speak, because unicorns don't have a spoken language, unlike your dragon friends."

Dan: "How did you know about them?"

Unicorn: "Well that would be telling. I'm not here to talk about them. It's you I wanted to speak to. What are you going to do about the situation you're in?"

Dan: "I don't have a clue; I'm so confused right now. What do you suggest?"

Unicorn: "I can't tell you what to do. You've got to make that decision for yourself."

Dan: "But how can I? Who do I trust now? The Jenoans I thought I could trust have let me down and the rest, well…"

Unicorn: "You just have to go with what's right in your heart and make sure you have a bit of fun along the way." Dan thought about it for a few moments.

Dan: "You're right. Thanks. I know just what to do. By the way, how do you know what's happened to me in the first place?"

Unicorn: "Your thoughts were deafening; I only came to have a drink, not get the story of your life."

Dan: "Yeah, sorry about that. I'll have to be more careful with my thoughts from now on."

Unicorn: "Just remember it's all about focus." Dan got up and after thanking the unicorn again, headed for Shonrar. The unicorn turned to walk away but hadn't got too far when Milo appeared in front of him.

Milo: "What did he have to say then?"

Unicorn: "Nothing, he didn't let anything slip other than what you told me. He picked up the focusing quite quickly; his other thoughts were like whispers after only being told once. Even you took longer to teach how to communicate telepathically efficiently."

Milo: "Did he give any indication as to whose side he was on?"

Unicorn: "No, but if he's indecisive you could help sway him your way."

Milo: "I'm going to try, but if I do succeed, Darkness will still destroy him eventually when I'm not around. You'd better go. We don't want to be seen together." But it was too late; Dan had picked up a presence approaching the unicorn on his Hader and had gone to make sure it was all right. He didn't want it to get hurt but he didn't want to discover it was working for Milo either.

Dan: "Well that makes it easier." He said to himself.

The City

When Dan arrived back in Shonrar, it was early the following morning. The sun had not yet appeared over the Snowy Mountains. He had needed time to think. As he approached the edge of the wood, he heard a rustling in the trees behind him and sensed something wasn't right. All of a sudden, someone jumped out of the bushes leaping towards Dan, who stepped slightly to the side. The jumper landed on the floor right next to him, stood up and said "I will get you one of these days you know." It was Mal. He and a few of the other boys were posted as lookouts. "We've just about finished here. We'll come in with you. It's good to have you back." Dan looked at his face and he knew he could trust him. They hugged and then turned towards the city gates. The boys were about to escort him inside when he told them to go on without him. "I'll be in soon, you go on without me." He looked at them walking in, waited until they were out of hearing range and then said, "What do you want?"

Darkness: "Just wanted to remind you about your end of the deal. Who's your friend?"

Dan: "No one. Is there anything else?"

Darkness: "That's not a nice thing to say. He didn't look like no one to me."

Dan: "Is that it?"

Darkness: "Just remember to keep your mouth shut; for his sake as well as yours."

Dan turned around, grabbed Darkness by the throat and pushed him up against a tree. "You better not do anything to any of my friends or the deal's off and you're back in the bottle… jar."

Darkness punched Dan in the stomach. He lost his grip from around Darkness's neck, bending over. Darkness then kicked him in the face. Dan was forced backwards. "Don't threaten me. I'm the victim here. You're the reason we're in this mess and it's your responsibility to get us out of it. So do as you're told and get us that Sceptre." Dan scowled at him, but Darkness gave a superior grin back. "Remember I'll be watching" Darkness said, pointing to his Hader and then slipping away through the trees. Dan headed back into Shonrar. He walked with Mal back to his apartment, but was very cautious about what he was saying. "So what time is training?" Dan asked.

Mal: "In about five hours. I'll come and pick you up from here." Alemap opened the door. "Dan! I thought I heard you." She flung her arms around him. "I was so worried about you." He turned to Mal, "See you later on then." Mal nodded, smiled and walked away.

Alemap: "Come in. You must be hungry." They walked into the apartment. "Come sit down. I'll make you something to eat and then you can tell me all about it."

Dan: "Do you mind if we don't. I'm tired and I have to be up for training in a few hours time."

Alemap: "That's fine; we can talk after that. You go get some sleep and I'll wake you for something to eat before you go." Dan headed for his room. "I'm just glad to have you back." He turned to face her and put on a smile. "It's good to be back." He walked into his room and lay on his bed, hugging his pillow. He didn't think he would sleep but he had been up for too long and his body just couldn't keep awake any longer. He yawned, rolled over and fell asleep.

Later that morning, Dan woke to hear Mal knocking on the door. He went to answer it but Alemap was already there. "Come in" she said, "Do you want a drink or anything?"

Mal: "Yes please." She made a cold drink and handed it to him.

Alemap: "Dan?" she turned around but he had already gone back in his room.

Mal: "I'll ask him for you."

Alemap: "Thank you." Mal headed for Dan's room and knocked on the door.

Dan: "Yes"

Mal: "It's me, can I come in." Dan opened the door enough to let him in. He was in the middle of getting changed.

Mal: "What happen to you out there?" he said looking at all the scars on Dan's body.

Dan: "I had a fight with Darkness."

Mal: "Darkness? I thought he was just a tale."

Dan: "Oh, he's real and working for Milo!"

Mal: "What, how did that happen?" Mal was gob smacked and sat on Dan's bed.

Dan: "Well, he was real enough to do this to me." Dan put his shirt on to cover up the bruises. "Don't tell Alemap though."

Mal: "You don't want her to worry, I understand."

Dan: "It's not that. I just don't want her to know." Before Mal could ask him why, Dan was out of the door. He walked straight through the main room towards the apartment door.

Alemap: "Don't you want any breakfast?" Dan didn't look at her but opened the door and shouted back "Don't have time, will get something later." Alemap looked at Mal who just shrugged his shoulders. Dan stood outside the door and turned to Mal and smiled "Are you ready then?"

Mal: "Yes, sure. Thanks for the drink." He quickly finished it off and left with Dan, closing the door behind him.

Dan: "I can do some cool new stuff with this Hader."

Mal: "Like what?"

Dan explained as they went to training.

Corey's Birthday

When training was over the boys and Christian went to the feasting hall where a surprise celebration had been set up for Corey's birthday. While he was talking to his family, the rest of the boys were in his eye line trying to make him laugh.

Ryan: "So the baby of the group has finally become a man."

Jordan: "About time, now we can all go to college."

Dan: "Not all of us."

Graeme: "What do you mean?"

Dan: "Well, I'm on my last task now. Hopefully when I've completed it, I can go home."

Ben: "But this is your home now." The rest agreed with Ben.

Dan: "I know, but I also miss my parents and friends at home."

Jake: "So that's it, we've only got you here for how long?"

Dan: "I don't know, but I might need your help." Everyone was saddened especially his best friend Mal.

James: "We'll do what we can, but for now let's go and get the birthday boy."

Matthew: "Birthday man now."

Lord Stephen was sitting at his table with a few of the other leaders. He called Dan over to him. "How did things go then?" he asked.

Dan: "Well I'm going to go back in a few nights time, because I heard them say they would be out. So I'm going to sneak back in then and get the crystal."

The Listening Device

In Milo's cave, he and Darkness were intensely listening to what Dan had to say and watching to make sure he didn't do or say anything that would ruin their plans.

Lord Stephen: "Oh, while I'm thinking the technician is over there and has something else to do to upgrade your Hader. In his rush, he forgot to install it and then he can initialise the upgrade." Dan didn't know what to do. "Why don't you give it to him now and he'll be done with it in a few moments." Lord Stephen got the technician to come over to him. Dan looked at the Hader and rolled his eyes. He took the Hader off and passed it over to the technician who took it back to his table with his tool kit on. As they were moving away, Milo and Darkness could hear Lord Stephen say something about how nice Alemap looked. When he reached the table Taylor started tinkering around with it. In the cave they could see Dan and Lord Stephen at times when the Hader faced them. They could see them talking but they were too far away for them to hear anything.

The technician calls over to them.

Taylor: "Do you know your Hader's being accessed from a remote location?"

Darkness began to panic. "Quick cut the connection before they find our location."

Milo: "Hold on a moment, see what Dan does first." Dan had to act fast. "No, that's fine, I know about it" he said and turned back to Lord Stephen.

Taylor: "Right. It's fixed now" he called, but Dan carried on talking so he got up and took it to him. Taylor approached the table.

Dan: "So I was talking with a unicorn."

Taylor: "Sorry to interrupt. Here you go I finished with it."

Dan: "Thank you." He put it back on his wrist.

Lord Stephen: "So you were saying about the unicorn." Milo and Darkness breathed a sigh of relief.

Darkness: "Do you think he's said anything to that boy?"

Milo: "To Lord Stephen, no he didn't have time to tell

him anything. But we should carry on watching just in case. What I'm worried about is the upgrade he's got and what extra function he now has. He could be able to cut the communication from his side, we'll see."

The Treasury

The celebrations went on into the night. Then at twenty past midnight, Dan made his excuses and headed for the treasury. As he went along the corridor, he talked to his Hader, assuming someone was listening. He was right they were.

Dan: "Right, I know that the guards change over at twelve thirty, so I'm heading to the treasury now but I'll only have about five minutes before the next ones arrive."

He stopped talking to his Hader when it indicated someone, Mal, coming towards him.

Mal: "Where are you going; the party's just getting started?"

Dan: "I'm just going for a walk. I'll be back soon." Darkness was watching and called his father in. "He's going to the treasury now. You see the one he's talking to now." He pointed to Mal.

Milo: "Maddox's son, Mal, yes what about him?"

Darkness: "They've been hanging around together all night and Mal follows him wherever he goes."

Milo: "Yes, so?"

Darkness: "So maybe we need some insurance to make sure Dan doesn't do anything he shouldn't." Milo smiles at his son. "I'll arrange something now. Any particular reason you picked him?"

Darkness: "Why should there be?" They smiled at each other and then Milo left while Darkness continued watching.

Dan: "You go back to the party, I'll be there soon. I'm just going to stretch my legs."

Mal: "I'll come with you."

Dan: "No, I wouldn't want you missing out on all the fun. I've requested a song for you. Go back and see if you can guess what it is."

Mal: "OK, see you soon, don't be long." Mal went back to the party.

Dan: "That was close," he said to his Hader.

Dan approached the treasury quietly. While he waited for the guards to leave he looked at how he was going to open the door. There were two bolt locks on the outside. He would have to be careful that they didn't make a noise and would have to bolt them up before anyone returned. When they did leave, he let them get to the end of the corridor before he made his move. Dan pulled the bolts back, ever so quietly, and made his way into the treasury, leaving the door slightly ajar. When he entered the room his Hader went off.

Darkness: "What's happened?"

Milo "Don't worry, it's just a security thing. His Hader will come back on as soon as he leaves the room with my sceptre. He doesn't know there is an anti-transmitting device within the treasury, a similar device to what they use in prisons so prisoners can't transport out. We have no worries about him leaving."

In the treasury, Lord Stephen came out from hiding when Dan called him. Dan quickly explained to Lord Stephen what was happening. "OK, I've got to be quick so listen carefully and ask questions later. First off, meet me here again at this time tomorrow and you can't tell anyone about this. I need to return Milo's sceptre to him. It's the only leverage I have at the moment. Darkness is Milo's son, whom he brought back from the dead. I know about what happened and how Darkness died, but we can talk about that later. I have to go back tomorrow night after I have been in here to get the Sceptre, at which time I'll get the purple crystal. You will then need to get the Jenoans of Shonrar to move into the Sandy Mountains above us, but do it quietly; we don't want anyone to know. Tell Lilechem there are some secret tunnels in Leychr leading to the Sandy Mountains. The Leychrians will be returning through these tunnels and will then attack Lilechem and Shonrar. So once I have left, get everyone else out of Shonrar into the Sandy Mountains. Do you know from the technician where the cave location is?"

Lord Stephen: "Yes"

Dan: "Good. Meet me there with the Shonrar army. We will follow the Leychrians through the tunnels. All of Lilechem needs to be hiding in the Leychr castle. My guess is the Leychrians will leave for battle as soon as they enter Leychr. Let them all go, we will fight them when they return. The Shonrar army should have reached Leychr by then. I'd best be leaving."

Lord Stephen: "OK, I've got everything"

Dan: "Oh and as well as finding me the sceptre, find out all you can about something called the Yashel Crystal and how exactly the purple crystal will help us. What it can do, how to destroy it, that sort of thing? OK. Quick, hide, I have to go."

Dan leaves the treasury empty handed. He locks the door and runs out of sight as the new guards approach from the corridor. Once out of the way, he looks at his Hader and apologises. "I couldn't find it, but I can try again the same time tomorrow. I've searched half of the room and I know where it's not, so I should find it tomorrow if it's in there. I'd best be getting back to the party before someone misses me."

Darkness: "Yeah, your little lap dog. So what do we do now?" He asks, turning to his father.

Milo "He's still got another night. Once he's done that, we can sort out a battle they'll never forget. He may be right though."

Darkness: "What about?"

Milo: "The sceptre may not be in the treasury, at least not in Shonrar. Send several shadow beings to Lilechem to look through theirs. We can't afford to wait for Dan to search through that one as well. It's much larger. If it is there, tell them to leave it. We can get it when we pay them a visit."

Party Aftermath

The next morning training took place as usual, alongside the daily tasks and everything seemed normal to everyone but Dan. He was worried whether he had told Lord Stephen enough, whether he had told him too much, how he was going to clear the city and if he could pull it all off without Milo or Darkness finding out. They weren't having much luck finding the sceptre in Lilechem either. The shadow beings reported no sign of it in the treasury. After a long night and then a worrying day, during which he couldn't share his concerns with anyone, Dan was looking forward to getting the night over with. He knew this might be harder than it sounded. He was hoping to have the backup of the Shonrar and Lilechem armies, but Dan was worried he may not make it to the battle. He knew that he would most likely be killed by Milo or Darkness before he could use the weapon that he didn't even have his hands on. To do what was required, he needed to get away from Alemap for a while, so he and Mal went out by the lake in the Shonrar woods for a bit of peace and quiet.

Mal: "What's wrong, you've been really quiet lately."

Dan: "I know something and… well I was happier being in the dark."

Mal: "What is it, can I help you?"

Dan: "No, not really. I think I need to sort this out for myself. I really would love to tell you, but given the situation and who it affects I can't."

Mal: "It's fine; you can tell me when you're ready or not at all. Just know I'm here to support you."

Dan: "Thanks, you're a good friend."

Mal: "I don't want you to leave."

Dan: "I don't want to go. I wish I could have both worlds or take you home with me. You could live with me, my Mum and Dad and my sister."

Mal: "You have a sister? I didn't know that."

Dan: "Yes, Cynthia, she's older than me. She used to look out for me before I came here. I've had you lot instead; nine brothers."

Mal: "What will you do?"

Dan: "I don't understand."

Mal: "Well, when you go back, they'll be older and you've grown up. Won't it be awkward?"

Dan: "I suppose. I don't know how I'll handle it. Probably just turn up on their doorstep claiming to have amnesia." They stopped taking about each other's lives before they met and talked about some of the fun times they had experienced over the years. The late afternoon passed into early evening.

Mal: "Do you think we should be heading back now?"

Dan: "Yes, I suppose we should." They set off back to the city. "Thanks for just now. It's just what I needed."

Mal: "My pleasure. So what was up with you and Alemap? Can you tell me that or not?"

Dan: "Well, without going into too much detail, she's been lying to me."

Mal: "About what?" Dan agonised again whether or not to tell Mal, but decided that he could let him know a little bit.

Dan: "When I first arrived here, I killed someone."

Mal: "Killed someone, what are you on about?"

Dan: "Seriously, I came here in a flame. That flame entered Phosia and I… I don't know, landed on a boy from here. He was only our age, but he was burned to death." He began to get upset. "I don't remember much about it, but the kid I killed is Darkness."

Mal: "Really, that's… well it's… I don't know what it is."

Dan: "He's out for revenge on me."

Mal: "What are you going to do?"

Dan: "There isn't anything I can do really." After a while they reached Dan's apartment.

Mal: "If you need anything let me know."

Dan: "Thanks, I will." He hugged Mal goodbye. "See you later." Dan went into the apartment. Alemap wasn't there so he went to his room to have a sleep.

The Awful Truth

At eleven o'clock that night Alemap returned. Dan was just waking up from his sleep. He heard her come in so went out to see her.

Alemap: "Hey, how are you feeling?"

Dan: "Fine."

Alemap: "What do you want to eat?"

Dan: "It's OK, I'll make something myself."

Alemap: "No, don't be silly I'll do it."

Dan: "I think I can make myself some food."

Alemap: "OK, what is it? You've been irritable for days. What's wrong?"

Dan: "Like you care."

Alemap: "Of course I care, just tell me what's going on." Dan finally couldn't take it anymore and had to tell her what he was feeling towards her.

Dan: "I'm a murderer because of you. Who knows how many Jenoans have died because of us. I killed Darkness or whoever he was before. I stole Milo's son from him and you didn't tell me. I've lived here for fourteen years oblivious to the fact."

Alemap: "I… I…"

Dan: "What? You what?"

Alemap: "I think we should go and talk with Lord Stephen."

Dan: "Why? What does he have to do with anything? Does he know about this too? Am I the only one who's been kept in the dark? What does he have to do with it? Tell me."

Alemap:	"He's the one who sent for you and who chose Milo's son to die." Dan calmed down slightly as he was shocked at the news.
Dan:	"Why?"
Alemap:	"He had no other choice."
Dan:	"You always have a choice; he just made the wrong one."
Alemap:	"I think we should go find him and Christian and talk this out."
Dan:	"I don't have time for this."
Alemap:	"Where are you going?"
Dan:	"Away from you" she grabbed hold of his arm as he started to walk away. He looked at her for a moment and when she didn't let go, he pulled his arm away. "Leave me alone." He walked out the door and headed for the treasury. Alemap ran out after him, but when she couldn't catch him she went to find Christian.

Return To The Treasury

Dan arrived at the treasury with time to spare. He sat himself down and leant against a wall. While he waited for the change-over, he thought of all the good things Alemap had done for him, opening up her home, looking after him and being his mentor. When it got to half twelve, the guards left down the corridor and Dan sneaked back into the room.

Dan:	"Right, let's get on with this. What do you have for me?"
Lord Stephen:	"Are you OK, you seem a bit stressed?"
Dan:	"I am and I have issues at the moment, but this

isn't the time or the place."

Lord Stephen: "OK, here is the sceptre. The purple crystal can be used as a shield. When mixed with a certain chemical, the user can create a protection bubble around them or others. If you get the crystal, we can do the rest. The Yashel Crystal is a catalyst for extracting a Jenoan's essence; once extracted it can be used for different things."

Dan: "Like keeping Darkness in his new body."

Lord Stephen: "It is a very dangerous item in Milo's hands, but it was originally designed for some other purpose."

Dan: "Which is?"

Lord Stephen: "We don't know, but it was meant to be used for good."

Dan: "That might be why I felt so strongly drawn to it. It felt good, but I thought it was a trick, you know like drawing a moth to a flame."

Lord Stephen: "Yes, but we can't let Milo use it against us. We may not be able to stop him."

Dan: "Quick, how about the plans for getting everyone out of the city once I've left?"

Lord Stephen: "We have emergency procedures set in place already. If I set those in motion then the city can be fully evacuated in about thirty minutes."

Dan: "Good. That will give me chance to get away from the commotion before Milo or Darkness sees it on my Hader. Right, I will see you on the Sandy Mountain later then. Listen; don't let anyone near the location of the cave until I give the all clear. Stop about two miles away; you'll know when there are any Leychrians or Jenoans around from your Hader. Darkness shouldn't be able to sense you that far away. I must go. See you later my friend."

Lord Stephen: "Dan, thank you, for everything. I owe you a debt of gratitude." Dan nods and leaves the room.

As Dan exits the room, his Hader comes back on and Milo is delighted to see his sceptre in Dan's possession. He has managed to get hold of a Hader himself and modify it to suit his needs. Milo contacts Darkness on his Hader. "Dan has the sceptre and is just coming out of the room now. Get it for me and use it to get the boy."

Darkness: "Yes father. I won't be long now."

Darkness ends communication. He is seconds away from the corridor Dan uses to get to the treasury. Dan has finished bolting the door again. He grabs the sceptre from where he is holding it between his legs, and goes back across to the corridor. He can sense Darkness as he runs, but when he gets round the corner runs into Mal.

Dan: "What are you doing here?"

Mal: "I followed you as I thought you might be able to use me to…" he looks at what Dan is holding "help steal from Shonrar? What are you doing?"

Dan: "I'll explain later, it's not what it looks like, trust me. We must get out of here. Darkness is here, somewhere near!" They run to the next corridor where Darkness is waiting for them. He grabs the sceptre and punches Dan in the face. Dan falls to the ground. Mal grabs hold of the sceptre and he and Darkness struggle over it. Dan is getting to his feet when Darkness manages to prise it from Mal. He pushes Mal against a wall, winding him, and flips the sceptre so it is upside down, smacking Dan on the head with the metal end of it, knocking him out. He then flips it back on Mal and pokes him with it. The stone on the end of the sceptre glows. Darkness tells Mal, who is about to lunge for him, to stop; pick Dan up and follow him. Mal loses all power to resist and goes along with Darkness' wishes.

The Battle

Mal The Drone

When Dan comes to, he is back at the lake in the Shonrar woods. Darkness is throwing water over his face to wake him. He sits up in shock from the cold water and then grabs his head. "My head."

Darkness: "Yeah, yeah. You're going to have a headache. Come on let's get up the mountain; father is expecting us." Dan looks around and gets to his feet. Mal is standing there in silence with a blank expression on his face. "What have you done to him?" Dan begs.

Darkness: "Don't worry, it's not permanent. Mal bring Dan with me." He said to Mal, who obeyed him immediately. Mal began pushing Dan in the direction of Darkness, who was running for the mountains. When they reached the mountains Mal became less pushy with Dan. Darkness noticed this. "Mal, climb up the mountain." Mal does this and Darkness turns to Dan "Hurry up and get up the mountain before your little friend here snaps out of it and falls down the mountainside."

Dan: "Why?"

Darkness: "Once the effects wear off and he comes back round, his body will go into shock for a few moments. You don't want that to happen while he's half way up the mountain, do you?" Dan hurries up the mountain behind Mal, hoping to catch him if he falls. After a while, they reach the top and head for the cave where Milo is waiting.

Darkness: "Mal, go inside and sit next to the crystal with the swirling colours." Dan is following Darkness who stops to talk to his father. He turns to Mal first. "Go on in then." Dan goes inside and sits with Mal, trying to get him to snap out of his trance.

The Yashel Crystal

Outside, Darkness hands the sceptre to Milo.

Milo: "I've missed this." He said spinning it in his hands. "So, you know what to do?"

Darkness: "Yes father. Just take enough energy from him to weaken him, then send him on his way with whatever item he wants, but keep the other boy as insurance."

Milo: "That's right and remember, if you want him to suffer then make sure his hands aren't touching the Yashel Crystal. It just draws the process out for a bit longer."

Darkness: "Have fun with the little puppies and set them on some nice Jenoans for me."

Milo: "I will see you later son. It's a new day and one we won't want to forget. Play nice with your friends in there. I'm off to find Rechly and get this thing started." Milo heads off into the Sandy Mountains.

Darkness: "It's a shame my father doesn't have the sensing powers I do or he would have known you are already here. What do you want Rechly?" He turned around and looked at the roof of the cave where Rechly was perched staring down at him. He jumped down next to Darkness.

Rechly: "I just want to have my way with those Jenoan boys; a bit of revenge for my brother Teburnt."

Darkness: "OK, I didn't see the point in sending them back with a weapon that could destroy us anyway. Wait here until I have drained his life force and then you can have his body, but the other we need to keep for now." Rechly stayed where he was while Darkness re-entered the cave. He found the two of them sitting on the floor together. "Well, isn't this sweet. If you can drag yourself away from your boyfriend for two minutes then we can start." Dan got to his feet and walked over to the crystal. "So what's Rechly here for, to make sure we don't escape?"

Darkness: "Something like that. Now if you want to get your hands on something else in the room, apart from your friend, then let's get started. Put your hands up to the crystal, actually just hold them a slight distance away from it." Dan did what he was told. He looked back at Mal one more time before the process began. Mal was still a bit dazed but was starting to come out of his trance now. Dan lowered his hands before Darkness could start.

Dan: "Can he hear what is being said to him?"

Darkness: "What?"

Dan: "Can he hear what is being said to him and understand it while he's like that?"

Darkness: "He understands me when I give him an instruction. I don't know about you. Now put your hands back up." Dan put his hands back up but before Darkness could begin he lowered them again. "Will he be alright now, he's not going to have a spasm or anything is he?"

Darkness: "Put your hands back up now, or I'll slit his throat and feed him to Rechly." He had such intensity in his eyes that Dan believed every word he said. Dan put his hands back up and Darkness quickly started. Dan couldn't break free when the crystal turned black. He was helpless to do anything.

Mal Comes To

After a minute of the process, Mal recovered from his mindless drone state. He saw what was happening to Dan, stood up and grabbed a cloth to throw over the crystal. The Yashel Crystal stopped and returned to its coloured state. Darkness and Dan took a few seconds to snap back to reality. Mal used this time productively to punch Darkness in the face, until he fell to the floor. He turned around to Dan who was staring at an exposed part of the crystal. Mal slapped his face a little and then covered it up. "Come on Dan, wake up, we have to get out of here."

Dan: "I'm here; I'm just strangely attracted to the crystal."

Mal: "Quick, let's smash it while we have the chance."

Dan: "NO. I mean, no, we should find the purple crystal and then leave. We need to get out of here before Darkness comes to. Look through that cupboard there" They start rummaging through Darkness and Milo's things. "Nice punch though."

Mal: "Yeah, but my hand hurts now."

Dan: "Your hand hurts? Look at mine." He raised them up to show Mal the scars left by the essence drain. "I'm starting to look like Jesus. You know, I was sure I'd seen it in this thing before. They must have moved everything around. Nothing looks familiar apart from the cabinet." Dan ran his hand over a mark in the cabinet, made when Alemap's knife had hit it after penetrating the mirror.

The Back Room

As they were searching, Mal found it hidden at the opposite side of the room and turned to tell Dan who was looking at his Hader.

Mal: "Got it, let's go."

Dan: "That's brilliant, except Rechly's heading this way and I think Darkness has woken up." Sure enough Rechly was tired of waiting and had decided to come in to see what the hold up was. Darkness was getting to his feet when he entered the room. Rechly looked around.

Rechly: "Where are they? They didn't come this way, past me." Darkness focused for a second. "They're in the other room down there. They're trapped. Hungry? I think it's snack time." Rechly licked his lips and bounded into the room. When they got in there, Dan and Mal were standing at the other side of the room looking quite smug. Mal was leaning on Dan's shoulder.

Mal: "Are you sure this is going to work?"

Dan: "There's only one way to find out." Darkness stood there, confused about why they were so confident, but Rechly was consumed with hunger for the two boys and ran at them full force. Dan stood confident as Rechly approached, while

Mal squinted a bit. When Rechly reached them they were surrounded by a purple bubble, which he couldn't stop in time to avoid. He ran into it and was thrown backward. He flew through the air into the other room, taking Darkness with him. They were both knocked out. Mal and Dan both entered the main room.

Mal: "Right, now's our chance to escape, while they're unconscious." Dan walked over to the crystal, stepping on the bodies of Darkness and Rechly on the way.

Mal: "Come on Dan, what are you doing? We need to get out of here." Dan just stared at the crystal. Mal grabbed him by the arm; pulling him away from it and around the bodies. But as Dan went past, Rechly grabbed his leg and bit him. Dan turned to him and kicked him in the face with the other foot. He fell back down on top of Darkness.

Dan: "Bad puppy. Go back to sleep." Dan and Mal left the cave. "I can't. We have to go back to the Yashel Crystal. Here you take this." He handed Mal the purple crystal.

Mal: "What do you want me to do with this?"

Dan: "Take it to Lord Stephen and the others. I'm going back in."

Mal: "No, they'll kill you, especially without this. I'm staying with you." Dan thought for a moment. I know what I have to do. He took his Hader off and threw it back in the cave. "Right, now we can talk properly. Come on we'll hide over there in the rocks until they go."

Mal: "Why did you get rid of your Hader? We need it and all the things it can do."

Dan: "Yes, but we don't need Milo and Darkness keeping tabs on us. It's been bugged. Quick, lets go." From their viewpoint, Dan told Mal everything he knew up to then. "So you see why I couldn't tell you anything. I so wanted to, but I couldn't."

The Cave & The Tunnels

In the cave, Darkness awakes to find Rechly sprawled across him. He throws him off. Rechly starts to come around too.

Darkness: "Damn it, they've gone."

Rechly: "Shall we go after them?"

Darkness: "Yes, in a minute. We don't want them giving the weapon to the others."

Rechly: "Let's go then."

Darkness: "Hold on, I want to see where he is first."

Rechly: "How?"

Darkness: "We tampered with his Hader." Darkness looks at the screen but can only see a wall. "I don't get it. Where is he?" Rechly went to the mouth of the cave. When he came back in he noticed the Hader on the floor. He looked into it and said, "It's over here." Darkness was shocked when Rechly's face came on screen. He nearly fell over. He sighed deeply "Well, we'll just have to head for the tunnels then. Come on let's go." They leave the cave and head to the tunnels.

Mal: "So what do we do now? Won't Lord Stephen be waiting for us?"

Dan: "Well, yes but if everything's gone to plan we shouldn't have anything to worry about. I never gave an exact time and he knows I might not have made it out at all."

Mal: "So are we going to follow them to the location of the tunnels?"

Dan: "Erm no!"

Mal: "Well how are we going to find them?"

Dan: "I'm hoping we can put our tracking skills to good use."

Mal: "Won't he be able to sense you here?"

Dan: "Yes, I think he'll sense I'm around but I'm not after him. At least not yet, so I'm not a threat. I think while I'm not doing anything which could hurt him, he can't pinpoint me from this distance." Dan peeped back over the rock. Mal pulled him back down.

Mal: "What are you doing, you're going to give our position away."

Dan: "I need to see the general direction they're heading for the tunnels. If they're heading towards us or Lord Stephen's location then we need to be worried." He peered back over. "It's OK now, they're heading that way. Huh, they really do look like a man walking his dog."

Mal: "What is a dog?"

Dan: "It doesn't matter. They'll probably go out of their way, thinking we're following them so we've got time now."

Mal: "To do what?" Dan smiles at him and holds his hand out to help Mal to his feet.

Dan: "Come on, this way."

Dan's Plan

The two of them head back for the cave. Dan's Hader is still on the floor. He walks around it trying not to be seen on the screen and they are both quiet so as not to be heard. The Hader, which has deactivated itself, is only in the entrance so they talk normally when they get to the main room. Dan begins looking through the room again.

Mal: "Why are we back in here? Are you looking for another weapon to help us? Isn't the Hader offline now anyway?"

Dan: "The Hader may not work, but the bugging device might. No I'm not looking for a weapon, and I don't believe that is a weapon anyway."

Mal: "Why not, you saw what it did before with Rechly."

Dan: "Yes, but it didn't so much perform as a weapon but as a barrier. I'd class it more as protection than weaponry."

Mal: "So the real weapon you find to use against them is still somewhere in here."

Dan: "Yes, I think so. Damn, I bet they took it with them."

Mal: "What? Do you know what it looks like?"

Dan: "Yes, I think the Yashel Crystal is the key here."

Mal: "You mean the swirly thing from before?"

Dan: "Yes, that."

Mal: "It's over there." He said pointing to it hiding under some bits of wood in the corner.

Dan: "Excellent." Dan picks it up in the cloth and takes it back to the stand where it was before.

Mal: "I don't know about this. It's evil. You know what it did to you before, why would you want to use that? I can see you're still drained from what he's done to you."

Dan: "Because nothing is totally evil, everything and everyone has some good and bad in them. That's the problem, we only focus on the bad things no matter how much good we do." He said removing the cloth. "The bad things are what stick in our minds. Sometimes you've just got to forgive and try to forget. I've felt the good energy in this and you're right, I'm too weak to fight otherwise."

Mal: "Are you upset about Alemap and the rest lying to you? Is that what you mean, forgive and forget?"

Dan: "I suppose."

Mal: "So, how do you use this thing?"

Dan: "I'm hoping I just put my hands up and say the magic words."

Mal: "Which are?"

Dan: "Izzy Wizzy, let's get busy."

Mal: "Nothings happening."

Dan: "Sorry I was joking about those words. It's something from Earth I used to watch with my father. OK, so I'm going to do this and then after half a minute throw a cloth over it to stop it. If it's good, I'll carry on, if not then we can destroy it, deal?"

Mal: "Deal, but be careful." Dan raised his hands to the crystal. He stood there for a few moments looking into it and then turned to Mal, holding the cloth and smiling. "Here goes nothing, or everything...'Come to me!'" The swirls in the crystal changed from slow moving to fast. Dan stood there unable to move. After twenty seconds, Mal threw the cover over it.

Mal: "Dan, are you OK?"

Dan: "Fine. It's good. I can feel it. This is why I've been so attracted to it. It is something powerful, but it's been trapped in here for so long."

Mal: "OK, keep going but I'll keep bringing you out after a bit so we can be sure."

Dan: "There's no time. Who knows how long it's going to take to free the magic from the crystal? I need you to go and find Alemap and the others. Tell them to go ahead with the plan and I'll join them as soon as I can, but avoid this area just in case."

Mal: "But what if you take the good and then the bad comes with it. You won't be able to stop by yourself."

Dan: "It's a chance we'll have to take. Besides, you know I'm a bit naughty anyway." They smile and Mal laughs at him.

Mal: "Fine, but be careful."

Dan: "I will. Track down the tunnels and go through. It's time to show these lot what Jenoans are made of!" Mal leaves and Dan starts up again but this time he puts his hands on the crystal.

The Hader

Milo contacts Darkness on his Hader. "I've just checked in on our friend Dan, but I can't see or hear anything."

Darkness: "Yes, he got away with the purple crystal, father and he got rid of the Hader in the cave before he left, I'm sorry."

Milo: "Don't be. That was the plan anyway. Do you still have his little friend?"

Darkness: "No, they escaped together."

Milo: "No matter. It doesn't affect the plan. When you leave will you bring me…?"

Darkness: "Father, I've already left. Me and Rechly are almost at the tunnels."

Milo: "Rechly's already with you? Can I guess what you two had planned? Oh, but if you're not at home then whose was the shadow on the wall of the cave when I checked before the Hader went blank? Never mind, carry on. I will see you soon. It will probably have been a shadow being looking for us." Milo continues with his campaign as Darkness and Rechly reach the tunnels. Rechly enters but Darkness stands outside looking back the way they had come. Rechly comes back towards him.

Rechly: "What is it? Are we being followed?"

Darkness: "No, I don't sense him at all now. That's what's worrying me."

Rechly: "Good! We've lost him, let's go."

Darkness: "No, you go. You will get to Leychr in half the time without me."

Rechly: "What are you going to do?"

Darkness: "I'm going hunting."

The Swirls

While Dan has been using the Yashel Crystal, only the red, yellow and orange swirls have been prominent. After the set of swirls moved from the crystal to Dan, the process stopped. A few moments later Dan was back in control of his senses. He felt different and the crystal had changed. After a couple of minutes, he put his hands back around the crystal and began absorbing the blue and green swirls, which became more intense as his hands approached the crystal.

The Tunnels

Under the leadership of Lord Stephen, all of Shonrar had been deserted. The Jenoans exited the city up to the Sandy Mountains. They headed through the mountains until they were only a few miles away from the coordinates given for Milo's cave. There, they pitched their tents and waited for the signal to carry on. They had brought their full battle gear and food to last them a week. After waiting there till morning, Mal joined them and passed on Dan's messages. They packed up camp and then headed past the cave and found the tracks Rechly and Darkness had made. These tracks led them to the tunnels through to Leychr, but one of the trackers pointed out that only one set led into the tunnels, while the other headed back in a different direction, but not directly where they had been coming. Mal was worried Dan might be in danger so he hurried back to the cave on a griffin. Lord Stephen took the rest of Shonrar into the tunnels and they began their journey to Leychr.

Darkness Prevails

Dan had been going all night and was just finishing extracting the last set of swirls from the Yashel Crystal. Darkness had returned to see him standing there, helpless. He went and fetched a sword from the back room. When he returned, he plunged it into

Dan from behind, just as the last of the blue and white swirls entered him. He fell to the floor, knocking over the stand the Yashel Crystal was on. It fell off the top of the stand and shattered. Darkness stood over Dan's body smiling to himself. He was about to leave for the tunnels when Milo contacted him.

Milo: "Are you OK son?"

Darkness: "Yes, why?"

Milo: "Because Rechly has arrived in Leychr and you haven't. I thought something had happened to you."

Darkness: "Oh no father, everything is brilliant from this end."

Milo: "Where are you now then?"

Darkness: "Erm, I'm back in the cave. I forgot something."

Milo: "Right, well, we are ready to attack now. I'm going to lead the attack on Shonrar while Rechly takes the other half of his troops to Lilechem. Come down the mountain and meet us at the lake in the Shonrar Woods. It's time we did some father and son bonding and take the city together."

Darkness: "I'll be there soon." He took one last look at Dan and headed to the entrance to leave for the woods, where he saw Mal standing by him with his sword drawn. He laughed.

Mal: "What's so funny?"

Darkness: "I didn't even sense you. Shows how much of a threat you are to me."

Mal: "What have you done with Dan?"

Darkness: "Ah, you see that's the other thing I can be happy about. My killer has been put to rest."

Mal:	"What?" Mal swipes at him with his sword. Darkness dodges out of the way.
Darkness:	"Now, we can stand here fighting all day when you know you've no chance or you can go see if your boyfriend has enough breath left in him to tell you he loves you." Mal drops his sword and runs to find Dan. Tears are in his eyes. He goes into the part of the cave where he left Dan and finds him lying on the floor. Mal knew he was dead, but felt for a pulse. He sat there mourning his friend when Darkness sneaked up behind him. "Did you not get a goodbye kiss?" Darkness stomped his foot on Dan's back and wrenched his sword out. He flipped his wrist so the sword spun around three hundred and sixty degrees and then held it at Mal's neck.
Mal:	"Go on, do it."
Darkness:	"Not got anything left to live for? How pathetic. I haven't come to kill you. After your father and now Dan, you're dead inside." He leaned in closer. "I want you to live with your pain; like I did." Darkness stood back up. "I only came back for my sword. Get a new hobby, like revenge. It's so much more exhilarating. Got to go, bye" he smiled and ran out of the cave. "We'll meet again old friend."

Mal got to his feet and ran to find his sword. He went outside but found no trace of Darkness. He got back on his griffin and headed back to the tunnels. When he arrived the last of the Shonrar Jenoans were going in. The passageway was only just big enough to get two Jenoans on a griffin through at a time. Mal entered, followed lastly by the guards set to protect the rear. He had only been going through the tunnel for a few minutes when he got a message from Ryan to meet him and the others at the

Shonrar Lake as soon as possible. Mal turned his griffin around with great difficulty and exited back out of the tunnel and down the Sandy Mountains towards the Shonrar Woods.

War Of Silence

In Shonrar, all was quiet. It was midday and Milo, Darkness and their troops had just arrived. They entered the courtyard by breaking down the gates.

Milo: "I thought they would have put up more of a fight than this. Where is the mighty Shonrar army now?" He turned to his warriors. "Burn them out." They lit up some torches and hurled them onto the buildings, instantly setting them alight. Each of the courtyard buildings was spaced apart so they had to be lit individually. Milo used his sceptre to shoot fire onto the buildings. "Oh, I've missed this!"

Darkness: "Where are they?"

Milo: "We probably missed some scouts out in the woods or we tripped some alarm. We'll head for the city centre and see what we can do." They continued to the centre of the city, but no one was to be found.

Milo: "Do you sense anything?"

Darkness: "No, nothing. Something isn't right here."

Milo: "Check the houses" Milo commanded, "check everywhere, kill anyone you find and toss their bodies out onto the street." The Leychrians broke into the houses, their roofs covered in grass, trees and flowers. They tore the places apart and stole what they could carry but they did not find a soul to put out on the streets.

Milo: "Where are they all hiding?"

Darkness: "I've checked and they're not in the great hall or tower either."

Milo: "You've been here, mingling with them over the past few years. Did they mention anything about a hiding place big enough for all of them?"

Darkness: "No. I can't think where they could be. It's like they've just vanished. So what do we do now?"

Milo: "We contact Rechly. Rechly?" he shouted into his level three Hader.

Rechly: "Yes?"

Milo: "What's happening?"

Rechly: "We are just raiding the houses here. They're all hiding somewhere, but we'll find them eventually. We won't leave a stone unturned."

Milo: "When you finish, report back to me."

Darkness: "Let's ride on, father and I'll see if I can sense anything." Milo and Darkness set off with hundreds of warriors hard on their heels.

Lord Stephen and the others had reached the Oasis underneath the Shonrar wood. They were travelling through the tunnels when they felt some cool air reach them. Further ahead, the tunnel had broken down in parts and the moving city could see the underground cave with the water flowing down from above. Lord Stephen decided they could all do with a break so allowed them to recharge their batteries and fill up on water, whilst keeping a strict eye on the time passing with his Hader. He was able to use it to navigate the general direction they were heading as his map was showing their location above ground. There were a few dead ends but in general they headed the right way and the scouts quickly took different tunnels to see how far they went.

The information about the tunnels was stored on Lord Stephen's Hader automatically, to provide assistance if he were to travel that way again.

By early evening, Milo and Darkness still can't find anyone anywhere and neither can Rechly and his army. They decide to head back to Leychr with their loot and work out where two whole cities full of Jenoans could have gone.

Victory?

Rechly's troops are the first to get back to the castle at the head of Leychr. They enter the home they left behind years ago, to what they believe to be a victory. As they pile in through the main gates to the castle courtyard, Rechly stops to make an announcement. He climbs to the top of the castle wall where he converses with his troops. "After fleeing our homes from these Jenoans we have finally come back to reclaim it as our own. And now we have them running scared. All of Shonrar and Lilechem are deserted. Tonight we will celebrate and tomorrow we will claim it all as our own. A new time for the Leychrians has arrived. No more must we stick to Leychr and cower around the Shonrar woods. From now on, they shall be known as the Leychr Woods." He is cheered by hundreds of warriors. "And now let us drink and feast and celebrate our return..." he turned away from the cheering to look at Leychr and said to himself "Home." He smiled and led the way to Leychr's main hall.

Hiding in the castle was the entire population of Lilechem. With the castle being totally deserted of any living thing, the Jenoans of Lilechem packed the castle from the dungeons, where the children and elderly were, right up to the chamber where the advance guards were. As the Leychrians returned home, they waited with baited breath for Julian, who had joined the Lilechem army for this battle, to give the signal to attack. Rechly opened the door to the inner grounds of the castle, which was once its city before the Leychrians arrived. They had left them unlocked before they went to do battle. As he flung them open and stepped inside, he felt something wasn't right. He took a few more steps followed by the vast army, itching to get into the celebratory mood after their wild goose chase.

Rechly: "Something's not right here" he muttered to the guards who had stopped behind him. He looked around but couldn't see anything out of the ordinary other than the city looking more run down than usual.

Then, from somewhere above him he heard a trumpet sound. This was the signal given by Julian to begin the attack. As waves of arrows flew from the darkness of the windows, hitting the unsuspecting victims below, Rechly commanded his legion to draw their swords to combat the soldiers appearing from the numerous doorways in front of them.

The soldiers of Lilechem advanced on to the Leychrian army. Those at the front were soon lying on the ground because of the blades of the Leychr warriors, their comrades having to scramble over their wounded and dying bodies. After a few moments, it was not just their bodies, which began littering the city but their opponents as they fought bravely to destroy the race that plagued their lands.

The Great Hall

Whilst those of the Lilechem city who were not fighting crammed themselves lower into the cells of the dungeons, the fighters were being backed into a corner as they retreated to the Leychr hall in order to regroup and to draw their enemy away from the Jenoans hiding away below. The Leychr soldiers took the bait but blocked off their routes of escape. Backing up to the far wall of the giant hall, surrounded by the hordes of Rechly's soldiers, the Lilechem troops were braced ready for attack. They were greatly outnumbered but were willing to go down fighting with their last breaths. Rechly came to the front of the pack.

Rechly: "Look everyone, our foods been delivered to us."

He was just about to tell them to tuck in, his mouth filling with saliva, when they were surprised by the arrival of the soldiers of Shonrar coming up on the Leychrians from all sides as they exited the tunnels in their attack formations. After being outnumbered by themselves compared to the Leychr army, which had expanded greatly over time, Lilechem's odds were evening out in their favour. Lord Stephen was leading the Jenoans of Shonrar to fight their way to those trapped in the hall, who now themselves got a second wind and advanced towards Rechly and the others.

Finding An Exit

As the battle continued, both sides had major casualties and the fighting was spreading into other parts of the kingdom. Lord Stephen contacted Julian on his Hader, but he was unable to talk as he was holding off enemies in the corridors by the dungeons. Julian managed to hold them off for a few moments by trapping himself and the others in a room, the Leychrians attempting to break down the door. This gave him the few moments he needed to speak to Lord Stephen.

Julian: "Everyone, get something you can use as a weapon. We may need to move from here soon." He used his Hader. "Yes my Lord?"

Lord Stephen: "We need to round this up quickly, before they have reinforcements from the group Milo is bringing back from Shonrar. Once we have finished here we must group together and head for them in the Shonrar woods." Julian was watching on his Hader but Lord Stephen was fighting while he was talking and the images Julian was receiving were of the floor, behind him and attacking foes.

None the less, he carried on with the conversation intent on getting the Jenoans to safety.

Julian: "I am with the Jenoans in the dungeon now, shall we move out?"

Lord Stephen: "Hold your position. We are making our way to you now. Wait for my signal." It went quiet on the other side of the door for a few seconds, when the door began to move off its hinges with the force of something behind it.

Julian: "They must have reinforcements; I have to go we're under attack again." He ended communication.

Lord Stephen: "Hurry" he said to the soldiers surrounding him, "we have to get to them quick, they are in trouble." The soldiers in front of Lord Stephen broke down a door in front of them that they had previously been unable to open. He was shocked to find Julian and the other Jenoans on the other side, poised for attack. As soon as the door opened, Julian went towards it, then stood a little way from it, to allow it to open and to see the dangers behind. He too was shocked, but extremely pleased to see Lord Stephen.

Julian: "Well, I wasn't expecting you."

Lord Stephen: "Me neither. I thought you were in the dungeons."

Julian: "We are. These are the corridors connecting them."

Lord Stephen: "Right, well the majority of the Leychrians have been wounded or killed in battle. There is still fighting going on in parts of the castle but most of them are retreating and heading to the Snowy Mountains behind Leychr."

Julian: "What shall we do?"

Lord Stephen: "Stay here in the castle with the Jenoans. We will flush out as many of the Leychrians as we can into the mountains. I will leave you some of my soldiers. Clear the bodies of the dead into the courtyard of Leychr. Put the Jenoans and the Leychrians at separate ends. I'm sure Lilechem will want to take their dead home. I know I want ours to be given a proper goodbye in Shonrar. Meanwhile, I want you to set up guards at the far end of the castle so that any Leychrians thinking of returning will be killed."

Julian: "We can't wipe out the whole race of them though, my Lord. The ones in the mountains are few compared to us. It seems unfair, maybe even cruel to kill them for returning to their home."

Lord Stephen: "We only need to keep them away so they don't provide the others with back up and so they stay away while we clear our Jenoans out of here. Then we shall let them back to their kingdom. Besides, they did the same thing clearing out our fellow Jenoans when they took over here."

Julian: "That's true, right good, I shall arrange things for you now."

Lord Stephen: "I will gather the troops and those from Lilechem to advance on Milo's returning Leychrians; they shall be here in a matter of hours otherwise. We want to fight them on our terms and on our ground. See you soon my friend. Be careful."

Julian: "You too my Lord."

The Ambush

As the Lilechem and Shonrar armies were entering the Shonrar Woods to attack Milo and the remainder of Rechly's army, Mal joined the rest of the boys at the Lake.

Mal: "What are we doing here?"

Ryan: "We're laying an ambush. Hopefully we are going to lure Milo and Darkness our way so that Lord Stephen and the others only have the Leychr warriors to worry about."

Graeme: "It was Dan's idea. Where is he?" Mal grew sad again and the others knew it was bad news before he told them.

Mal: "He's dead."

Ben: "No! He can't be! What happened?"

Mal: "Darkness ran a sword through him."

Corey: "I don't believe it."

Mal: "It's true. He stuck it through him from behind and left him to die." They all stood in silence for a few moments while they absorbed the fact they would never see their friend again.

Jordan: "We will avenge his death. We must make sure Milo and Darkness are stopped, even if it means fighting to the death."

Matthew: "It probably will now. Milo has his sceptre. So what can we do?"

James: "We need to get it from him for a start, and then we can attempt to kill them."

Mal: "At least, we need to disable them long enough for the others to defeat the army. It won't be easy for them, they are still outnumbered."

Ryan: "How? There were never this many Leychrian before."

Jordan: "They have obviously been breeding while they've been away."

Matthew: "So Mal, what does Lord Stephen say about all this?"

Mal: "He doesn't know."

Corey: "What do you mean, he doesn't know? Does he know Dan's dead?"

Mal: "How could I tell him that? They've been placing all their hopes on Dan fulfilling his supposed destiny to help us win this battle. He was supposed to find this weapon for us to use against them to tip the scale in our favour but now he's gone, there won't be any hope for them."

James: "Mal's right. They need to believe Dan is still alive so that they can finish this."

Jake: "Maybe Dan is the weapon."

James: "What do you mean?"

Jake: "Well, maybe the weapon that the legend is on about isn't a physical one but an ideal, which gives the rest of us a reason to fight."

Mal: "He shouldn't have lost his life so that we could live though. He never asked for any of this. He was brought here and trained to do their dirty work for them. He's been destined to die since he arrived on Phosia with all his ridiculous tasks."

Ryan: "Mal, calm down. He lived a happy life. When we were together we all had fun didn't we?"

Matthew: "I don't mind reminiscing on the life of our friend but shouldn't we be discussing ways in which to lure Milo and Darkness to where we want them?"

Mal: "You're right we must avenge Dan's death. So what are we going to do?"

Shadow Informant

As they talked, a shadow began to move away from the clearing. It sped through the night to Milo and Darkness returning to Leychr at the back of the army.

Shadow: "Master, I have news about the young ones."

Milo: "What is it?"

Shadow: "They are planning to ambush you."

Darkness: "Ten… sorry, nine of them, just waiting to be slaughtered. They have no chance. Can I, father?"

Milo: "Hold on, why are they so confident?"

Shadow: "Well, between them and the army coming from Leychr they are still outnumbered, but they do seem to manage to win when we have attacked them in the past."

Darkness: "Hold on, what army? Rechly, that snivelling weasel! He's betrayed us father."

Milo: "Quiet boy, we are with hundreds of his troops who are loyal to him. We don't want them turning on us now, do we?"

Darkness: "Sorry father, you're right."

Milo: "Besides I don't believe the army you are talking about is Rechly's is it?"

Shadow: "No Master, it is a mixture of soldiers from Lilechem and Shonrar."

Darkness: "Why would they be coming from Leychr though? Surely they will be caught by the troops there?"

Milo: "I think not my son. We know none of them were in Shonrar or Lilechem when we entered. They must have already been in Leychr when we came out of the tunnels or in the mountains behind. Otherwise we would have noticed them as we went to the cities."

Darkness: "I don't understand. How did they get there? How did they know?"

Milo: "I don't know but you can bet your life it's something to do with that meddling boy."

Darkness: "Well, at least we don't have to worry about him anymore."

Milo: "What do you mean?" Darkness looked down at the floor.

Darkness: "He was messing around with the Yashel Crystal when I was back in the cave. He was in a kind of trance so I took the chance to kill him." Milo pulled his griffin over to his son.

Milo: "Look at me. I'm not angry with you. He deserved to die. After all he killed you. Now it's time for the rest of them." One of Rechly's soldiers approached them. "Lord Milo" he said.

Milo: "Lord Milo, I like that. Go on."

Soldier: "We are under attack at the front of the army. What are your orders?"

Milo: "Carry on towards Leychr. Don't let anything get in your way."

Soldier: "Yes, Lord Milo."

Milo: "Shadow, where did you see the young ones?"

Shadow: "They were by the lake in Shonrar."

Milo: "Darkness, you and I shall go there and dispose of the young ones; with their children gone, the elders will be easy to defeat, we'll bring back their heads as proof."

Shadow: "But they are setting you up in a trap. Are you sure you want to go by yourselves."

Milo: "They will be expecting us to turn up. We don't want to disappoint them do we?"

Darkness: "Besides we can handle the nine of them between the two of us."

Shadow: "Very well. Is there anything you would have me do master?"

Milo: "Not for now, you may leave."

Shadow: "As you wish."

Surprise

The shadow being left them and they headed to the Shonrar Lake. Once they got there Darkness could sense the danger before they got near the lake. When they arrived, Milo put his sceptre down on the banking and he and Darkness took their griffins to drink.

Jake and Ryan were hiding, waiting in the same tree ready to attack.

Jake:	"They're here."
Ryan:	"A bit convenient don't you think?"
Jake:	"There must have been something that told them we were here? I thought I saw a unicorn earlier. Maybe it was that."
Ryan:	"Well maybe, but unicorns are totally impartial. They won't help Milo or Darkness as such. They're just nosy. They communicate with both sides and love to gossip."

Mal gave the signal and the boys surrounded the two in silence, or thereabouts. As Mal reached down for Milo's sceptre, Darkness shouted "now." He and Milo spun around to face their oncoming attackers. Milo held out his hand and the sceptre moved across the ground towards him, evading Mal's grasp. Milo spun the sceptre round in his hand, as did Darkness with his sword, a move taught to him by his father. He then brought it up in the air, pointing it at Mal. The crystal on top began to glow and Mal flew into the air. Unlike when Milo had thrown the Leychrians, he could send Mal flying further by channelling his power through the sceptre. Mal landed in some bushes far from the others. In their pairs, the boys took it in turns to attack Milo and Darkness. They kept coming until they were all on the floor. Mal was on his feet again and came back to the area where they were fighting.

Milo:	"Had enough yet?"
Darkness:	"No, we've just started. Can we play with them a bit longer before we kill them?"
Milo:	"If you like, but not too long. We need to make sure Rechly's army can handle the forces of Lilechem and Shonrar."

All the boys were now back on their feet but Mal signalled to them not to attack. He stood facing Milo and Darkness with the others at the sides of them. Milo looked at him and laughed while Darkness suddenly sensed danger.

Milo: "What are you going to do; take us on yourself? This will be funny."

Mal: "I'm not stupid; I won't take both of you on."

Darkness: "No! They have help…but it can't be!"

Milo: "What is it?" Mal stepped to one side and Dan walked out from the trees.

Dan: "It's only little old me."

Milo: "You! I thought you'd killed him?"

Darkness: "I did."

Dan: "Well, I just couldn't leave without saying goodbye. Hi Mal."

Mal: "Hey Dan."

Dan: "So, who do you want, Milo or Darkness?"

Mal: "I think me and Darkness have a few things to sort out."

Dan: "You heard him boys, you lot versus Darkness and I'm fighting against Milo."

A New Dan

Milo and Darkness both had worried expressions on their faces. Dan approached Milo while Darkness ran and jumped over the boys and headed into the woods. The boys followed him.

Milo pointed his sceptre at Dan and threw him in the air. Dan went flying but landed gracefully on the ground. Milo was stunned. Meanwhile, the boys surrounded Darkness, attacking him in a similar pattern as before, except this time he didn't have his father to help.

Milo sent Dan flying away again when he got near to him.

Once again Dan landed on his feet, but this time he had a few tricks of his own. Dan lifted his hand and flicked it sideways. Milo stared for a second as nothing seemed to happen but then the sceptre flew out of his hand and into the lake. Dan then flicked his hand again, but upwards and Milo's eyes opened as he was thrown to the other side of the lake.

Darkness, seeing this, began to fight more intensely. He managed to escape the boys for a moment and headed for the lake.

Milo, lying on his back, sat up and looked at Dan who was heading towards him. He walked over to edge of the water. He put his hands together as though he was praying and then split them apart. As his hands opened, the lake moved to either side creating a path for Dan. He walked across this and ended up on the banking at the other side. Darkness had now reached the lakes edge and was about to cross, when the water went back to normal. A lot less confident than before, Milo drew his sword and Dan drew his, whilst on the opposite side, the boys had caught up with Darkness.

Milo: "So you're still alive. How did you do it?"

Dan: "It's a gift." They struck swords and Dan's Hader activated, showing him a memory.

Rebirth

When Mal had left the cave, the elements that Dan had absorbed from the crystal protected him from dying. They also repaired his wound. Dan had come round lying face down on the floor. He was a bit dazed and wondered what had happened. His Hader had activated and filled in the blanks. He remembered the Yashel Crystal, and sensing Darkness behind him, but couldn't do anything. He remembered the pain of being stabbed in the back and then looking down at the Yashel Crystal, which was now empty and looked like a large crystal ball. The next thing he remembered was waking up on the floor.

Dan came out of the memory and no time had passed. He and Milo had their swords clashing together.

Milo: "So how did you survive? Darkness told me he'd stabbed you."

Dan: "That's right. I thought I was dead." He explained as they whirled their swords at each other "I don't really know what happened but I think it was something to do with that Yashel Crystal you introduced me to." Milo's face changed as he clicked to what must have happened.

Milo: "The weapon!"

Dan: "Yeah, we all thought the purple crystal was something to do with me, but it turns out it can be used for something better." Dan turned around to his friends across the way and shouted, "Activate your crystals boys."

The Purple Crystals

Each of them stood back from Darkness, who was worried about what they were about to do. They pulled out some water and poured it onto their belts, on which they all had a fragment of the purple crystal attached. A purple light immediately surrounded them and faded after a few seconds. Darkness lunged for the nearest two boys with his sword and a knife from his leg holster. As the weapons hit the bubble, they retracted off it and the bubble glowed again, becoming visible for a few seconds. He went to pick up his sword and started slashing away at the boys who didn't move and had their swords by their sides. It was no use, he couldn't get his sword anywhere near them.

Dan: "Thanks for the purple one; it's quite cool, used in protection. As I'm sure you already knew which is why you let me have it. You knew it wasn't 'the weapon' and I thought it was."

Milo: "Well, I knew it was a powerful object but I didn't know what it was used for."

Dan: "It was lucky as well, because we found out how it worked from being in your cave. When Rechly came to attack us, we knew the crystal was already working. It was being dripped on from your leaky roof. We saw the bubble go up, but then it disappeared and we thought something had happened, like it had run out of power. We were looking for weapons and Mal picked up a rock. There were only a couple in the room, so we knew we couldn't do much with them. Mal threw it at the wall in anguish but it bounced back and the bubble activated as it approached me."

Milo: "I don't get it though. How did you know what we were planning?"

Dan: "When you went into the other room, after breaking the connection between me and Darkness, I was thinking to myself that I wished I could hear what you were saying." Dan knocked Milo to the ground. "This was before I could move much, so I sat and listened as my upgraded Hader put your conversation on a louder volume. Then, once you saw me moving to the door, I switched it off so you couldn't hear yourselves echoing into the room, then back on when I went back until you came through."

Milo: "So that's how you found out, but one of us was watching and listening to you the whole time. You didn't reveal anything to anyone about our plan. Although, I thought you would to your little friend over there."

Dan: "No, I said everything I needed to say to Lord Stephen."

Milo: "When the technician messed with the Hader?"

Dan: "That's right."

Milo: "But you only had a few minutes. There's no way you could have told him everything you needed to."

Dan: "I didn't tell him anything then. I told him later."

Dan's Hader showed him the memory of him and Lord Stephen talking while Taylor updated his Hader.

Dan: "Right, I only have a short time until he brings it back, you have to listen I need your help. Is there anywhere we can meet up alone later to talk?"

Lord Stephen: "Yes, of course, come to my quarters…"

Dan: "No, it has to be somewhere that my Hader won't work. I'm being watched by Milo and Darkness on it."

Lord Stephen: "Well, it won't function in the guard's station, the special weaponry room, the treasury..."

Dan: "The treasury, that's fine." The technician calls over to them.

Taylor: "Do you know your Hader's being accessed from a remote location?"

Darkness began to panic. "Quick cut the connection, before they find our location."

Milo: "Hold on a moment, see what Dan does first." Dan had to act fast. "No, that's fine, I know about it" he said and turned back to Lord Stephen. "That's them. OK, what time do the guards change after midnight?"

Taylor: "Right, it's fixed now" he called, but Dan carried on talking so he got up and took it to him.

Dan: "So I'll meet you there then, alone. Be out of sight so they don't see you. Oh and try to find out from this guy if he knows the remote location he was on about. You'll need it later." Taylor approached the table. Dan sensed him approaching and started a new topic "so I was talking with a unicorn."

Taylor: "Sorry to interrupt. Here you go I've finished with it."

Dan: "Thank you."

Lord Stephen: "So you were saying about the unicorn." Milo and Darkness breathed a sigh of relief.

Darkness: "Do you think he's said anything to that boy?"

Milo: "To Lord Stephen, no he didn't have time to tell him anything. But we should carry on watching just in case."

Darkness' Choice

Milo: "So what happens now?"

Dan: "Well, we'll take you two back and lock you up. Possibly throw away the key."

Milo: "We're not going to spend the rest of our lives locked up." He stood up and began to run away. Dan looked at him and used his powers to build a wall of earth from nowhere, in front of Milo, which he then ran into it and knocked himself out.

The purple crystals began to dry out and the purple shield lit up and broke up from the top leaving the others exposed again.

Darkness knew this was his chance to get back to winning. He quickly tripped up the approaching attacks until it was just he and Mal. Darkness tackled Mal and managed to get his arm around his neck. He then used him as a shield. The other boys got to their feet. Mal pulled a knife out, but Darkness saw it and swiped it off of him. He held on to Mal and got the others to back off. They couldn't get near enough to help Mal so they backed off. Ryan called out to Dan to help. They all turned to him and Darkness turned his head also, in time to see his father run into the mud wall. He turned back to the boys who were edging in on him.

Ryan: "Do something Dan."

Dan looked over. He didn't do anything. Darkness turned with him and Mal so he was facing Dan. He had the knife up to Mal's throat and made the others stand in front of him with their backs to the lake. Dan came back across the lake by jumping clear over it.

Dan: "OK then Darkness, let him go and come with me."

Darkness: "Are you kidding? As soon as I let go you'll kill me."

Dan: "No, I won't. That's your style not mine." He let Mal go for a moment, but held the knife at his back. "Don't move anywhere." Mal stayed where he was.

Dan: "Let him come to me and everything will be alright." Darkness was really anxious.

Mal spoke out. "If he wanted to kill you, he could have when you had your back turned."

Darkness: "Why didn't you?"

Mal: "He wasn't going to stab you in the back, he's not a coward."

Darkness: "Don't start with me; remember who has got a knife to your back right now."

Dan: "Mal don't." Mal shut up "Let him come to me Darkness and you walk away with your father, start over somewhere new, there's no need for you to kill anymore it's over."

Darkness: "How do I know I can trust you?" Mal was about to say something but remembered all too well about the knife poking him in the back.

Darkness told Mal to start walking slowly towards Dan. He did do. He got half way between Dan and Darkness, when Darkness panicked. He raised the knife above his head and threw it at Mal. Dan screamed and raised his hands as the knife flew through the air at Mal. He created a hole in the ground with one hand and Mal fell into it. With the other hand, a ball of fire shot out and hit Darkness in the chest, killing him instantly. He raised Mal out of the ground. Then he looked down at his own chest to see the knife stuck into his heart. He fell to his knees and toppled onto his side.

Milo had seen parts of what had happened to his son, for the second time. He had heard Darkness beg Dan not to kill him and Dan agree. He was then getting to his feet and turning towards them, when he saw Dan kill Darkness, this time intentionally. He was distraught. He tried to scream, but no sound came out of his mouth. He turned away and left, before the boys came after him and before seeing Dan fall to the floor.

Saving Dan

Scrambling to his feet, Mal runs over to Dan's motionless body. He pushes his way past the other boys and puts Dan's head in his lap. He feels for a pulse again but cannot find one. The others can tell from his face this is it.

Corey: "Can't we do something? What happened last

time before he came back?"

Jordan: "Yes, try thinking of what we can do to make it work."

Ryan: "Make what work?"

Jordan: "Whatever it was that made Dan come back to life last time."

James: "I don't know, but didn't he say something about taking his sword out."

They all think back to when they saw Dan return. Dan had seen them by the Lake, when the shadow being had left. They were discussing their tactics, when he just appeared from the wood. Naturally, all of them had their mouths to the floor.

Falcons: "Dan!"

Dan: "Hi."

Mal: "We thought you were dead!"

Jake: "No, you thought he was dead and we all believed you." He said punching him in the arm.

Dan: "He was right. I think I was dead."

Matthew: "Then how come you're here?"

Corey: "Are you a ghost?"

Dan: "No." One of the boys goes over and pokes him to make sure.

Graeme: "No, he's real. Hold on, Milo hasn't reanimated you so you can kill us has he?"

Dan: "Ah, you found me out." He drew his sword. They all backed off and drew their swords when Dan started laughing. He put his sword away. "I'm only messing with you. Put them away."

For a second they didn't know whether to believe him or not. They had always played childish pranks on each other when they were around each other, but they knew Milo could know that too from using the Yashel.

Dan: "No, really I am alive."

Ben: "Prove it."

Dan: "How?"

Ben: "I don't know."

Dan: "Oh, I do. Look my Haders working." He put his arm up and showed them the location of where they were.

Ben: "What does that prove?"

Ryan: "It proves he's alive because if his body was dead for longer than five minutes, the Hader self destructs or something."

Mal: "So you must have come to just after I left."

Dan: "I heard you and Darkness talking and you running towards me but then it all went black. I felt my life slip away. It was really weird."

Jordan: "So how come you're alive now?"

Dan: "I have no idea how, but I'm sure it was something to do with that Yashel Crystal and what I've absorbed from it. Oh and by the way did you take the sword out of my back?" he said to Mal.

Mal: "No, Darkness did."

Dan: "I wondered where it had gone. I stood up and felt my back for the sword but it wasn't there and neither were you or Darkness. Look, I don't even have a scar where it went through me." He showed them.

Ben: “So if we remove the knife maybe he’ll heal again?”

Mal: “Maybe, but maybe not. He did just absorb all the Yashel Crystal before. That might have had something to do with it.”

Corey: “Oh, come on, just pull the damn thing out.” He leaned over Dan’s body and pulled it from his heart before anyone could stop him. Though they weren’t sure and didn’t want him to do it, once he had, they glanced down at Dan’s wound to see if anything happened.

Ben: “Nothing, now what do we do?”

Corey: “Give it chance.” Mal was tearful and couldn’t really see what was happening in Dan’s body but the others had all gone silent. Mal wiped his eyes and glanced down to see a host of swirls emanating from Dan’s wound. A few seconds later they stopped and the wound was gone. Dan opened his eyes and sat up.

Dan: “Hey, what happened? Never mind, just got a flashback. How long was I out for?”

Mal: “A few minutes.”

Dan: “Where’s Milo?”

James: “He ran off into the woods.”

Dan: “Where’s the sceptre? Never mind I know where it is. Help me up.” Dan walked over to the Lake and raised his hand up. The others stood by him as they watched the Sceptre rise up out of the water. Ryan picked it up and handed it to Dan.

Dan: “Right then Falcons. What say we go help the rest of them finish this battle?”

They began walking to their griffins to head for Leychr. Mal was sharing a griffin with Dan. He sat behind him.

Mal: "So how did you do all that stuff before?"

Dan: "I don't know. It's kind of like using a Hader. It activates when I need it. I just knew what I had to do and it happened. Cool huh?"

Mal: "Very. Glad you're not dead, again."

Dan: "Thanks. You too, guys." he said to the others. They then rubbed under the griffins armour so their wings would grow and flew on to Leychr. When in the air, Dan looked over at the Sandy Mountains to Milo's cave and smiled. Mal asked him what he was smiling for.

Maverick's Trap

When a moment arose in the battle, Maverick and a team of soldiers sneaked away and headed towards Milo's cave, thanks to the co-ordinates supplied by Dan. Once there, he and the others searched for specific items they believed were to be used by customers of Milo. The items they did find, they bugged in order to monitor the devices whereabouts and see who was being supplied with what. The others left him installing the final pieces to his devices and headed to their griffins, a fair distance from the cave. They then patiently waited for Maverick, who was struggling attaching a tracker. He heard a noise and quickly hid. It was Milo returning, distraught over his son's second death. After smashing a few things, he headed into the back, giving Maverick the chance to escape and run for the griffins. He picked a tracking device off the floor from one of the smashed items and hoped there weren't any more lying around. Darkness's essence returned to the cave to see Maverick leaving. His father had the Yashel and was calling for him. He entered it and Milo set about preparing to insert him into a new victim by calling upon a shadow being to get a victim for him.

The End Of The Battle

The battle raged on into the early hours of the morning, but with their leaders gone, the Leychrians were fragmented and were driven away easily. Dan and the Falcons reached Leychr and helped to get the bodies of their dead and Lilechem's to their appropriate cities.

Goodbyes

Dan returned to Shonrar and to Alemap's apartment. She had been so worried about him and embraced him when he walked through the door.

Alemap: "I'm so glad you're alright. I'm really sorry we… I didn't tell you the truth about your past but I didn't want to hurt you and…"

Dan: "Don't worry about it. I do understand. I'm not happy about what happened, obviously, but I know you had everyone's futures in mind."

Alemap: "It doesn't make a difference. We should have found another way to get you here, but until the technology was available, we had to use magic to bring you."

Dan: "OK, let's not talk about it; after all I can't talk. I saw what was going to happen to Mal and I reacted and now Darkness is dead, again."

Alemap: "Do you want to talk about it?"

Dan: "Not right now. I was just upset with myself that I had let him down."

Alemap: "Who?"

Dan: "Darkness; he wasn't going to hurt Mal I believe that. I think he panicked. He was outnumbered and everything was against him. I should have got the other Falcons to back off a bit, give him some space but I didn't and now… both times were my fault."

Alemap: "Come on let's go."

Dan: "Where?"

Alemap: "You'll see." Dan really wanted to go to sleep, but he left with her and they headed back to the sacrificial area he had arrived at. All the Falcons, the Shonrar leaders and Lord Stephen were there. On the floor was a chest that they were all gathered around.

Dan: "What are we doing back here?" he said getting bad feelings from them.

Alemap: "Well, we've come to say goodbye."

Dan: "What? We're having the funerals here? Is that a bit tacky?"

Lord Stephen: "No, we will give them a proper goodbye later. We've come to say bye to you."

Dan: "What? I'm going now, this minute? I never got to go to the beach."

Mal: "We don't want you to go yet but if you don't go now…"

Dan: "What? I can't ever leave?"

Mal: "No, I was going to say it'll be harder."

Lord Stephen: "You have fulfilled your duties to us," he said in an official voice "and now you may return to your home world." He smiled, "but seriously we're really pleased you came and we're really going to miss you. So with the help of the MPC we've managed to give you a present." He pointed to the box.

Dan: "What is it?"

Christian: "It's a box."

Dan: "I can see that. What's in it?"

Lord Stephen: "You'll find out." Lord Stephen, Christian and Alemap all looked suspiciously at each other.

Dan: "Oh no, let's not go through this again. What's in the box?"

Lord Stephen: "In the chest there isn't anything. It's just a secret compartment at the moment. It's what is going to be in the chest that is interesting."

Dan: "Which is?"

Christian: "When you leave here, the box will hold your powers within it. You can't take the chance that when travelling home through space, something will sense your new powers; they're much too strong. You could either be captured, or lead some unknown species back to your planet. You don't want that."

Alemap: "So when you arrive back, all you have to do is open the chest and your powers will be returned to you."

Dan: "I get to keep my powers, sounds alright what's the catch?"

Alemap: "Apart from the fact you need to open the chest as soon as you reach Earth, there is no catch. We will put a Hader in the box for you so we can keep in contact."

Dan: "So what do I do now? Oh and will it take all my powers or just the new ones?"

Lord Stephen: "Yes, your sensing power will be mostly taken from you. A bit will remain but not enough to alert anyone or anything on Earth. All you have to do is call the flame to take you back home again. Once in the flame, place your hands on the box and you will be relieved of your powers."

Christian: "Just make sure you do it before you leave Phosia so you don't run into any trouble."

Present For Milo

Dan: "Well, I guess this is it then. Thank you all for having me here. I've enjoyed it so much, well most of it."

Christian: "We've loved having you here."

Dan: "So I suppose I'd better be off then, but before I do there is something I need to do." Dan closed his eyes. Everyone wondered what he was doing when his Hader activated and a map appeared before them. Dan was travelling through Phosia at great speed, using his mind. The onlookers could see him travelling through the Shonrar woods, up through the Sandy Mountains, to Milo's cave while still standing in front of them. What they couldn't see, but Dan could, was that Milo was using the Yashel Jar to try and bring back his son in another victim. All of a sudden, Dan opened his eyes and threw some fireballs towards the cave. They flew on the wind, over the trees and up the mountain into the cave, where they bounced off of the walls. The first fireball to reach the cave was the largest and Milo could do nothing to stop it. He could only watch on as it bounced around his home, destroying things in its path. Then, it headed straight for him. He dodged out of the way and it struck the Yashel Jar behind him. He turned to it on his hands and knees and tried to pick up the pieces, as his son's soul started to slip away. Meanwhile, more fireballs entered the cave. They hurtled towards the young man lying, tied up, on a table. They hit the ropes binding him and the young man was freed. He got up and ran out of the cave while Milo was distracted with the Yashel Jar.

Back in the clearing, Dan's Hader was now moving in reverse, at an equally fast speed, back to where he was. The Hader stopped.

Dan: "Right, that's that sorted then."

Mal: "What did you do?"

Dan: "Just made sure Milo won't be bothering you with his tricks again. Well, I must be going now." He looked up at the sky and raised his hands. The Jenoans with him all looked up but nothing happened. Dan lowered his hands.

Lord Stephen: "What's wrong, did it not work?"

Mal: "Are you going to have to stay now?"

Dan: "No" he said to Mal with a sad face, "I'm going. It's just going to take a few minutes to get here." In the few minutes he had left, he said goodbye to his friends.

Milo was crying outside his cave, ready to throw himself off the edge of the cliff. "I'm sorry I've failed you son." Darkness was floating around his father. "It won't be long before you're gone from this plain. There isn't enough time to get another Yashel Jar and the Crystal has been broken." His eyes were full of tears, but he saw a light coming from the sky. He rubbed his eyes and opened his arms thinking it was a final fireball, sent to destroy him. When he looked, it wasn't heading for him but back to the sacrificial area. “No! Darkness, quick you must get into the path of that flame. Follow Dan to his world and as you are entering its atmosphere, knock him out of the flame. When his body hits the ground, you should be able to enter it. If not, try one of his race. They won’t be protected by the MPC for that sort of thing so you won’t require a Yashel Jar or Crystal. Go quick, I will find some way of contacting you.” Darkness floated over towards the flames destination. Quickly, Milo turned and gathered a few devices and called for the shadow being to get him something. It arrived instantly and gave him a gun like weapon. Milo grabbed the weapon from him, looked at the device and then fired it at the items he had gathered. The gun shot out a small burst of light towards the items and they disappeared into it. Milo then ran outside and pulled down an eyepiece from the side of the gun. He looked through this towards the direction of the flame and calibrated the gun to the centre. He then flipped a switch on the weapon and fired it at the chest. The items from the gun were then shot inside the flame. Milo breathed a sigh of relief, but then noticed something on the floor. He looked closely at it and turned to the shadow being. “What’s this?” he demanded. “I don’t know” the reply came. Milo threw the item to the ground and stamped on it. “We have to leave now.” He grabbed a few things together and then fled into the Sandy Mountains, with the shadow being returning to his own kind.

The Flame

At the sacrificial area, Dan was saying his last goodbye to Mal. He sensed the flame was near and then they began to see it in the sky.

Dan: “Right then, I must be off.” He went and sat on the box. “So, to give my powers to the box, I just place my hands on it?”

Lord Stephen: “Yes, and want to give them away. Quick, throw us your Hader!” Lord Stephen, Alemap and Christian were backing everyone away from Dan so that they didn't get caught in the flame. Dan took his Hader off and threw it to Mal. "Don't forget me will you."

Mal: "I won't."

Lord Stephen: "You have a Hader and some weapons in the chest. Good luck Dan Wild."

Dan: "Thanks, you've all been great and best of all; in order for me to go, no one has to die this time. I won't forget you." Once again Dan was engulfed in the flame, which bounced back up into space leaving the ground scorched. The rest of the Falcons headed back to Shonrar City with a saddened Mal, as did the other leaders. All that remained in the clearing were Alemap, Christian and Lord Stephen.

Lord Stephen: "Yes, you will forget us."

Alemap: "We shouldn't have lied to him; after all, he won't remember when he gets back."

Christian: "No, he won't, but we didn't have time and we didn't want everyone else knowing did we?"

Alemap: "I suppose not."

Lord Stephen: "We've done the right thing. Besides, that won't be the last we see of him. Once he figures out how to mask his trail, he'll be back. He's only fulfilled his first prophecy. Next time he'll be more than ready for what's to come."

Alemap: "That's true." They all return to Shonrar.

SECTION 04
The Return Home

As Dan leaves in the flame, he is happy that he's helped the Jenoans of Phosia. Rechly's army has been defeated and his numbers greatly reduced. He knows if Rechly does return to Leychr his depleted numbers mean he won't be able to do anything to Shonrar or Lilechem for a long time to come.

As he gets near to the atmosphere of Phosia, Dan is about to renounce his powers when he senses something isn't right. "You've got to be kidding me." He senses it is Darkness and as they leave the planet behind, a struggle ensues. Within the flame, Darkness is tangible, although he doesn't have any distinct human or Jenoan features. He is still a floating spirit and tries ramming Dan out of the flame. Dan can move around in the flame but be stopped at the flames' edge. If he wanted to, from here he could break out of the flame or be pushed. He notices some items floating around in the flame with them, while outside they have picked up a tail. A round metallic looking ball is following the flame.

Back inside, the chest is floating around in the middle of the flame. Dan tries to keep the fight away from it. Darkness picks up on this and after failing to get Dan out of the flame, decides to push the box out instead. He knocks Dan over to one side and heads for it at full speed. On reaching it, he tries pushing it but as he touches it, the chest opens. Dan hurries over to him and the chest, but before he can reach them, the chest sucks Darkness inside with a Hader and another item sent by Milo. These items and Darkness are all in caught in the top section of the chest, while the items for Dan are in the secret compartment underneath. The chest closes itself. Dan tries to reopen it, but he can't. Realising that he is out of

Phosia, Dan quickly places his hands on the chest and gives his powers away, hoping that Darkness can't access them from inside. After a few moments, he feels the powers leave him. He is about to take his hands away when he realises something else is happening. Believing it is Darkness doing something; Dan fights desperately to remove his hands. He looks down at them to find them shrinking, but it's not just his hands. It is happening to his whole body. As he gets nearer to Earth, his body goes through a reverse transition of growth. As he approaches his home planet, the metal ball stops at a distance from the atmosphere while the flame continues in.

Dan's memories of Phosia begin to fade. He returns to Earth as he left, as a seven-year-old boy. Before he reaches his destination, he is freed from the chest. Being curious about its contents and not remembering about Darkness, Dan opens the chest and Darkness flies out. The flame, as before, bounces back into space but Dan emerges from it unharmed and after believing he has narrowly escaped death, calls for his dog, which runs to him.

As the flame leaves carrying the chest, Darkness is freed on Earth. He follows Dan but realises he has no idea who he is and that he will soon require a host to keep him anchored to this plain. When the flame leaves the Earth's atmosphere for the second time, the device sitting in space fires a beam at the chest. It is hurled from the flame back down to Dan's location. The box passes through the essence of Darkness, trapping him in it and ends up crashing into the back of Dan's fathers' shed. The doors had been left open and it hits the back wall, knocking things on top of it. Here it will remain hidden under junk, in the shed, for many years until someone finds and opens it.

After leaving the flame, Dan runs back into the arms of his loving parents, who take him back into the house, the dog following behind. His mother walks him in, while his father looks around to see if anyone is about. She comes back out alone. "Has anyone seen anything?"

George: "I doubt it. If so, we'll hear it on the news tomorrow but I think we've got away with it, this time."

Patricia: "Well, it's only just begun so we'd better be extra careful from now on." They both return into the house and shut the door.

END OF PART ONE

Glossary

Boozemises	Zombies
Ceprens	Keys to open time and space rifts
Ebaliy	Town in Jenon, Phosia
Falcons	Name given to the group for training
Jenoan	Species from Jenon
Jenon	Country in Phosia
Leychr	City in Jenon, Phosia
Leychrian	Species from Leychr
Lilechem	City in Jenon, Phosia
Phosia	Planet
Phosian	Species from the planet Phosia
Shonrar	City in Jenon, Phosia
Spencer Island	Island in Jenon, Phosia
Yashel	Group of items used to manipulate spirits

www.ingramcontent.com/pod-product-compliance
Ingram Content Group UK Ltd.
Pitfield, Milton Keynes, MK11 3LW, UK
UKHW041848190726
13854UKWH00002B/776